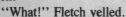

"Hello, Chief," Moxie said.

Chief Nachman said to her: "... silent—"

"What!" Fletch yelled.

"Will you please allow me to finish reciting this lady her rights?"

"You're arresting Moxie?"

"If you'd stop making so much noise."

"But you can't!"

"I can. I should, I must. I am arresting Ms. Moxie Mooney for the murder of Steven Peterman..."

FLETCH IS BACK AGAIN

to win new acclaim as he did
for *Fletch And The Widow Bradley*

"Fletch is one good reason the crime novel is alive and well."

—*Advocate,* Victoria, Texas

"Gregory Mcdonald is one of the most consistently entertaining mystery writers around. His newest novel [*Fletch And The Widow Bradley*] is no exception. [Fletch solves the case] with the same pared-down prose and sharp humor that have made Mcdonald's previous novels so much fun."

—*Times and World-News,*
Roanoke, Virginia

Books by Gregory Mcdonald

Running Scared
Fletch
Confess, Fletch
Flynn
Fletch's Fortune
Love Among the Mashed Potatoes (Dear M.E.)
Who Took Toby Rinaldi?
The Buck Passes Flynn
*Fletch and The Widow Bradley
*Fletch's Moxie

*Published by
WARNER BOOKS

FLETCH'S MOXIE

Gregory Mcdonald

WARNER BOOKS

A Warner Communications Company

FLETCH'S MOXIE

1

"What happened to Steve?" The woman in the canvas chair leaned forward. She had not looked around from the television screen since Fletch entered the pavillion. No one else was there. She was speaking to herself, or to the air. "For God's sake, what's wrong?" she said in a tight, low voice.

Even under the canopy on a sunless day, the screen of the television monitor was blanched by daylight from the beach.

From where Fletch was standing, he could see the pale images flickering on the screen. Across a few meters of beach, between the cameras, standing lights, reflectors, and sound booms, he could see the reality of what was on the screen, the set of *The Dan Buckley Show*, host and guests.

In the middle chair sat Dan Buckley wearing white trousers, loafers, and a light blue Palm Beach shirt. Even at a distance, amiability seemed stuck on his face like a decal. To his left, in a long, white bulky dressing gown sat Moxie Mooney—the gorgeous, perky, healthy, fresh-faced young film star called away from her make-up table to oblige an on location talk show. To Buckley's right sat Moxie's agent, manager, and executive producer, Steve Peterman in three-piece, pearl-gray suit, black shoes, and cravat.

Only Steve Peterman wasn't sitting properly in his chair. He was slumped sideways. His head was on his right shoulder.

Fletch looked at his watch.

At the back of the talk-show set a heavy, brightly colored, split curtain moved slightly in the breeze. Behind the set, down the beach the Gulf of Mexico was gray-blue in that light. On all sides of the set was the paraphernalia of a much bigger set, the location of the film-in-progress, *Midsummer Night's Madness*, starring Moxie Mooney and Gerry Littleford. Odd-shaped trailers were parked on the beach, each facing a different direction, as if dropped there. False palm-thatched huts were here and there. Thick black cables ran every which way over the sand. Low wooden platforms, like portable dance floors, were tilted on the beach. Strewn everywhere were the odd-shaped light rigs, reflectors, cameras, and sound cranes. The whole beach looked like a sandbox of toys abandoned by a giant, rich child. Among all these trappings moved the film crew of *Midsummer Night's Madness*, working, apparently oblivious of the taping going on in their midst.

"What happened?" the woman repeated in a hoarse whisper.

Fletch put his glass of orange juice back on the bar table. He stood quietly behind the woman in her canvas chair. She still hadn't looked around at him.

Closer, he could see the monitor more clearly. In a loose head-shot, Moxie was alone on screen, laughing. Then she looked to her right, as if seeking confirmation from Steve Peterman, as if turning the conversation over to him. Moxie stopped talking with a short, sharp inhale. Laughter left her face. One eyebrow rose.

The camera pulled back to include Buckley. He looked to his right, to see what had surprised Moxie. His eyes widened. His lips did not move.

The camera pulled back farther. Steve Peterman's eyes stared blankly into the camera. His head was at such an odd angle resting on his shoulder his neck seemed broken. Blood oozed from the lower, right corner of his mouth. It dribbled down his cheek past his ear and onto his cravat.

In the pavillion, the woman in the canvas chair screamed. She stood up. She screamed again. People everywhere on the beach, even on the talk-show set, were looking at her. She clasped her hands over her mouth.

Fletch took her arm. Gently, firmly, he turned her body toward him. Her eyes were affixed to the monitor.

"Come on," he said. "Time for a break."

"What's happening? What happened to Steve?"

"Coffee," he said. "They'll be right back."

He turned her away from the reality of what was happening on the set and away from the unreality of what was happening focused on the television screen.

"Steve!" she called.

He made her walk. She stumbled against the canvas chair. He pushed it out of her way with his bare foot.

"Come on," he said. "Let's see what the canteen has to offer."

"But, Steve..." she said.

She put her hands over her face. He put his arm around her shoulder and guided her along.

He walked with her off the pavillion and up the beach to the flat, hard-packed parking lot. There were many trailers parked there.

In a reasonable tone of voice Fletch said, "I don't think there's anything you can do just now."

2

"Is Steve Peterman your husband?" Fletch asked. He was careful to use the word *is* rather than *was* although he was sure the latter was appropriate.

In the metal folding chair, her drawn face nodded in the affirmative. "I'm Marge Peterman."

Fletch had found two metal chairs and placed them behind a trailer in the parking lot, out of the way of the traffic he knew would be passing to and from the beach. He sat Marge Peterman in one and went to the canteen. He brought back two cups of coffee, one black, the other with cream and sugar. He offered her both. She chose the black. He put the other coffee on the sand near her feet, and sat quietly in the other chair.

Fletch had arrived at the location of *Midsummer*

Night's Madness on Bonita Beach only a half hour before. His credentials from Global Cable News had gained him entry onto location. The security guard told him Moxie was taping *The Dan Buckley Show* and enjoined Fletch to silence. He directed Fletch to the hospitality pavillion where a courtesy bar had been set up to host the television crew and other press after the taping.

There he had found a woman sitting alone on a canvas chair watching her husband on a television monitor.

Now they were sitting together behind a trailer at the edge of a parking lot.

She had sipped her coffee cup dry and then picked the Styrofoam cup to little pieces. Bits of Styrofoam were in her lap and on the sand around her feet like crumbs.

"When are they going to tell me what happened?" she asked.

She could have rebelled from Fletch's ministrations and found out for herself. She didn't. She had understood enough of what she had seen to prefer acute anxiety to dead certainty.

"Breathe deeply," Fletch said.

She took a deep breath and choked off a sob.

The Rescue Squad ambulance was the first to arrive. Blue lights flashing on the gray day, it threaded its way slowly and carefully down onto the beach. A police car arrived next, its siren and lights on, but seemingly in no great hurry. Some local police had already been assigned to the film location. Then two more police cars came screaming, skidding in as if their drivers hoped the cameras were on. Out of the passenger seat of one emerged a middle-aged woman in uniform.

Marge Peterman said, "If they take Steve to the hospital, I want to go with him."

Fletch nodded. The ambulance had not returned from the beach, as it would have if there were any necessity to go to the hospital.

"I mean, I want to go with him in the ambulance."

Fletch nodded again.

Most of the people, the film crew, the television crew, the press, had gone down to the beach like pieces of metal being drawn by a magnet. Now a few were returning. As they returned, they walked with their chins down. Their shoulders seemed higher than normal. And the skin beneath their tans seemed touched by bleach. None was talking.

Fletch could not hear the murmur of the Gulf or even the chatter of the birds among the palm trees.

An airplane taking off from Fort Myers passed overhead.

A young woman in shorts, a halter, and sandals appeared around the corner of the trailer and stopped. She looked back toward the beach, wondering what to do, looking for support. A man with a large stomach extending a dark blue T-shirt, with dark curly hair, a light meter dangling from a string around his neck arrived and stood next to the young woman. He kept looking at Marge Peterman's back. A young policeman joined them. He shoved his hat back off his sweaty forehead and looked toward the road, probably wishing there were traffic to direct. One or two other people came to stand with them.

Dan Buckley came around the corner of the trailer and looked at each of the people standing there. He, too, hesitated. Then he slowly came forward and put his hand on Marge Peterman's shoulder.

She looked up at him.

"Dan..."

Fletch gave Buckley his chair and stood aside.

"Mrs. Peterman..." Dan Buckley said. "Marge, is it?"

"Yes."

"Marge." He leaned forward in the chair, forearms on his thighs. "It seems your husband...It seems Steve is dead. I'm sorry, but..."

Buckley's face lost none of its confident amiability in its seriousness, its sadness. Watching him, Fletch wished that if he ever had to take such bad news, it be broken to him by such a professional face as Dan Buckley's. In Buckley's face there was the built-in assurance that no matter how bad the present facts, there would be a world tomorrow, a show tomorrow, a laugh tomorrow.

Marge Peterman stared at Buckley. "What do you mean 'seems to be'?" Her chin quivered. "'Seems to be dead'?"

Buckley's hands cupped hers. "Is dead. Steve is dead, uh, Marge."

Her face rejected the news, then crumpled in tears. She took her hands from him and put them to her face. "What happened?" she choked. "What happened to Steve?"

Buckley looked up at Fletch. Then he sat back in the chair. His eyes ran along a heavy-duty cable strung over the parking lot.

He said nothing.

The young woman in the halter came forward and put both her hands on Marge Peterman's shoulders. "Come on," she said.

Marge stood up and staggered on the flat ground. The man in the blue T-shirt took her arm.

Together, the man and the young woman walked Marge Peterman through the trailers to the front of the parking lot.

"What did happen?" Fletch asked Buckley.

Buckley focused on Fletch. "Who are you?" he asked. Fletch was wearing sailcloth shorts, a tennis shirt, and no shoes. "The Ambassador from Bermuda?"

"Sometimes I get coffee for people," Fletch said.

Buckley looked over the bits of Styrofoam on the sand. "He got stabbed." He shook his head. "He got a knife stuck in his back. Right on the set. Right on camera."

"He was quiet about it," Fletch commented.

Buckley was looking at his fingers in his lap as if he had never seen them before. "It could not have happened. It absolutely could not have happened."

"But it did though, huh?"

Buckley looked up. "Get me a cup of coffee, willya, kid? Black, no sugar."

"Black no sugar," Fletch repeated.

Fletch walked toward the canteen, past it, through the security gate, got into his rented car and drove off.

3

The first phone call Fletch made was to Global Cable News in Washington, D.C. His call got through to that hour's producer quickly. It was, 'Yes, sir, Mister Fletcher', 'Yes, sir, Mister Fletcher' all the way through the switchboard and production staff.

Recently Fletch had bought a block of stock in Global Cable News. Just ten days before he had toured their offices and studios in Washington.

He had allowed everyone to know he was a journalist and they might be hearing from him from time to time.

"Yes, sir, Mister Fletcher," said that hour's producer.

Fletch looked down at his bare feet on the

rotten, sand-studded floorboards of the porch outside the mini-mart. When he was working full time as a journalist, no one in power had ever called him *sir*. They had called him many other things. He had always known, of course, that behind the power of the free press was the power of the buck. He had never felt the sensation of the power of the buck before. He decided he liked the sensation and that he must work to deprive himself, and others, of any such sensation. A *barefoot boy with cheek* should be listened to because he's got a story, not because he was able to buy a few shares in the company.

"'Sir'?" Fletch said. "To whom am I speaking, please?"

"Jim Fennelli, Mister Fletcher. We met last week when you were here. I'm the bald guy with the big side whiskers."

"Oh, yeah," Fletch said. Jim Fennelli looked like a stepped-on cotton pod. "The gumdrop fetishist."

"That's me," Fennelli chuckled. "A box a day keeps the dentist healthy, wealthy, and sadistic."

"You know *The Dan Buckley Show*?"

"Sure. My mother-in-law fantasizes she's married to the creep."

"They were taping down here on Bonita Beach this afternoon. On location for a movie called *Midsummer Night's Madness*."

"Cute. Prospero's Island in Florida."

Fletch said nothing. No matter how long he lived, he would be amazed at the great mish-mash of information, and misinformation, all journalists carry around in their heads.

"Have I got it right?" Fennelli asked.

17

"Sure, sure. On the set of the television show were Buckley, Moxie Mooney, and her manager, Steve Peterman."

"So? Mister Fletcher, are you trying to get a publicity shot for somebody? I mean, are you invested in the film, or something? I mean, anything regarding Moxie Mooney will fly, she's gorgeous, but where's Bonita Beach, anyway, north of Naples?"

"Yeah. More south of Fort Myers. Call me Fletch. Makes me feel more like me."

"That's a hike. We'd have to send people over from Miami. You stockholders, you know. Like us to keep our expenses down."

"Send people over from Miami. Steve Peterman was murdered."

"Who?"

"Peterman. Steven Peterman. Not sure if Steven is spelled with a *v* or a *ph*. On television, it doesn't matter how his name is spelled anyway, right?"

"Who is he again?"

"Some sort of a manager, a friend, of Moxie Mooney. Some kind of a producer of *Midsummer Night's Madness*."

"Yeah, but so what? Nobody knows who he is."

"You haven't got the point yet."

"My father lives in Naples. It's nice down there."

"He was stabbed to death on the set of *The Dan Buckley Show* while they were taping. While the cameras were running."

There was a pause on the other end of the line. "Yeah, that's good," Fennelli said. "You mean they don't know who did it yet? They will as soon as they look at the tapes. Fast story. A six-hour wonder. I'm not saying it's a bad story."

"Someone was murdered on camera."

"Yeah, but it wasn't a live show. It should be reported, of course."

"Obviously, both Moxie Mooney and Dan Buckley are suspects. They were the only ones within reach."

There was another pause while Fennelli marshalled in his mind his own camera/sound crew, on-camera reporter, his visuals, his story approach, his electronic pick-up.

The mini-mart was off the only road leading into Fort Myers Beach. Several of the cars and vans Fletch had seen in the parking lot of the *Midsummer Night's Madness* location had gone by on the road while he was on the telephone. As he was leaving the beach, police loudspeakers had been ordering everyone present to report to the local police station. Because of security on location, police would have the identities of everyone who had been there, of every potential witness. Among these names, they would have to have the identity of the murderer.

"When did this incident occur?" Fennelli asked.

"Three twenty-three P.M."

"Can we go on the air with this right away?"

"I'm sure AP radio news has already run it."

"What do we have they don't have?"

"Beg pardon?"

"You got a new angle to the story? Like, I mean, new news?"

On the road, a white Lincoln Continental went

19

by. Moxie was in the front passenger seat. Fletch couldn't see who was in the back seat.

"Yeah," Fletch said. "One of the prime suspects is about to disappear."

"Yeah? Which one?"

"Moxie Mooney."

The second phone call was to The Five Aces Horse Farm near Ocala, Florida.

"Ted Sills," Fletch said to whoever answered the phone. "This is Fletcher."

Fletch waited a long time. He ran his mind over the rambling ranch house, the swimming pool area, the two guest cottages, the stables, the paddocks, the tack room—all the handsome aspects of Five Aces Farm. At that hour of the day, Ted Sills would be in the tack room talking veterinary medicine and racing strategy over Thai beer with his trainer, whose name really was Frizzlewhit.

There was no breeze on the porch of the minimart. It was a gray, sultry day.

"Yes, sir, Fletch," Ted's voice finally boomed into the phone. "You coming by?"

"Just wanted to see if you're using your house in Key West."

"For what?" Ted Sills said. "I'm here at the farm."

"Then may I use your house in Key West?"

"No."

"Oh. Thanks."

"What are you talking about?"

"Want to get away for a few days."

"From what? You're always away. Where are you now?"

"Southwest Florida."

"You want to go to Key West?"

"Yeah."

"There are some nice hotels there."

"Don't want a hotel. Hate to be awakened in the morning by work-eager maids."

"So you don't have to make the bed. Hotels make your breakfast for you, too."

"Need a little p. and q."

"That mean peace and quiet?"

"It do."

"I need the nine thousand dollars you owe me in feed bills."

"That much?"

"The horses you have training here at Five Aces do eat, you know. A race horse cannot train on an empty stomach, you know. A race horse, like the rest of us, is encouraged by gettin' its vittles regular. You know?"

"You'll have it in the morning. Now, may I borrow your house?"

"The house rents for twelve thousand a month."

"Twelve thousand what?"

"Twelve thousand dollars."

"Twelve as in after-eleven-followed-by-thirteen?"

"The very same twelve. You're very good at figures, Fletch, except when it comes to writing them on checks for feed bills."

"You let me stay in The Blue House for free when you were trying to sell me some slow race horses."

"What do you mean, 'slow race horses'? You had a winner last week."

"Really?"

"Speedo Demon won the fourth at Hialeah. You should have been there."

"How much was the purse?"

"Let me see. Uh . . . Your share was two hundred and seventy dollars."

"Some race."

"Well, it was a plug race. And the favorite was scratched."

"Good old Speedo."

"She was faster than five other horses."

"Did the fans stay for the whole race?"

"Fletch, someone's gotta own the losers."

"Why me?"

"I expect they sense that you resent their feed bills. Horses aren't dumb that way. Race horses are like a certain kind of woman, you know. You gotta spoil 'em with a smile on your face."

"Okay. Feed the horses. But, damn it, Ted, make sure their overshoes are buckled before you put 'em in a race, willya?"

"We always buckle their overshoes."

"Now. About The Blue House."

"No."

"I only want it for a few days."

"Twelve thousand dollars. I wouldn't rent it for just a few days. Wouldn't be worth changing the bedsheets."

"You rent it very often at that price?"

"Nope. Never before."

"Uh, Ted . . ."

"I've never rented it before. I don't want to rent it. I put a price on it just because you asked. As a friend."

"Okay. As a friend, I'll take it."

"You will?"

"I will."

"Boy, no other sucker was born the minute you were."

"Make sure the bedsheets are changed."

"That's twenty one thousand dollars you owe me."

"So—some weeks are more expensive than others."

"Will I get the money?"

"In the morning. In nickles and dimes."

"You don't really care about money, do you? I mean, you have no sense of money, Fletch. I've noticed that about you."

"Money's useful when you have to blow your nose."

"Maybe I'll drop by, while you're there. There are a couple of other race horses I'd like to talk to you about."

"Don't expect to stay in your own house, Ted. You'll find the room rent very expensive."

"Naw, I'd stay at a hotel. I'll phone down to the Lopezes. They'll open the house for you. You going down tonight?"

"Yeah."

"I'll tell the Lopezes you tip well."

"Do. And tell good ol' Speedo Demon happy munchin' for me."

Fletch didn't need his credit card for the third phone call he made. It was to the airport in Fort Myers.

The man Fletch spoke to there repeated three times that Fletch was chartering a one-way flight from Fort Myers to Key West, with no stops. Which made it four times he said it altogether. There was something hard, almost threatening in the man's voice when he said *with no stops*.

"There will be no dope aboard the plane," Fletch finally assured him. "Except me."

Fletch pushed open the door to the mini-mart.

The woman behind the counter was Cuban. She looked at his smile and said with an impeccable accent, "How do you do? You need shoes to come in the store."

"Can you direct me to the police station?" Fletch asked.

Immediately, her face expressed genuine concern. "Is there some problem?" She glanced through the window. "Trouble?"

Fletch grinned more broadly.

"Of course."

4

The lobby of the police station looked like the departure point for a summer camp. The film and television crews sat around in various combinations of shorts, jeans, T-shirts, halters, sandals, boots, sneakers, sunglasses, western hats, warm-up jackets. Plastic and leather sacks bulging with their equipment hung from their shoulders and lay at their feet. Fletch had put moccasins on before entering the station.

The local press, two wearing neckties, stood in a clump in the middle of the lobby. There were lightweight sound cameras among them.

Fletch leaned against the frame of the front door.

All these various people engaged in getting various kinds of reality onto various kinds of film eyed each other with friendly distance, like members of different denominations at a religious convention. They were all brothers in the faith but they worshipped at different altars.

A few looked at Fletch curiously, but no group claimed him. He was not proselytized.

Around the room were a few familiar faces he had never seen before in person. Edith Howell, who played older women, mothers, these days; John Hoyt, who played fathers, businessmen, lawyers, sheriffs; John Meade, who played the local yokel in any locale. The young male lead, Gerry Littleford, sat on a bench along the wall in white duck trousers and a skintight black T-shirt. Like a well-designed sports car, even at rest he looked like he was going three hundred kilometers an hour. His lean body seemed molded by the wind. His black skin shone with energy. His dark eyes reflected light as they flashed around the room, seeing everything, watching everybody at once, missing nothing. The girl in the halter who had been kind to Marge Peterman was next to him, leaning against a wall, chewing a thumbnail. Marge Peterman was not there. There was a short, thin, weather-beaten man Fletch had not seen before, even on film, wearing some sort of a campaign hat and longer shorts than others wore. Fletch noticed him now because he was the only other person in the room who did not seem a part of any group.

The booking desk was to the left. Across the lobby from it, between two brown doors, was a secretary's desk. One door was labeled CHIEF OF POLICE, the other, INVESTIGATIONS.

The instant the door marked INVESTIGATIONS opened the two mini-cameras were hefted onto shoulders, unnaturally white lights went on, and the two men in neckties, holding up pen-sized microphones like priests about to give blessings, stepped forward. The other reporters followed them.

Her head neither particularly up nor down, her eyes looking directly at no one, Moxie Mooney came through the door and started slowly across the lobby. She was a saddened, concerned person momentarily oblivious to others, despite the light, despite the noise.

Using a Brazilian dance step which hadn't been invented yet and elbows which had had much practice, Fletch shoved forward with the rest of the press. The reporters were murmuring polite questions, *How do you feel? Will shooting continue on* Midsummer Night's Madness?

Fletch's voice was the loudest and sharpest of all: "Ms. Mooney—did you kill Steven Peterman?"

All the reporters jerked their heads to look at him and some of them even gasped.

Moxie Mooney's deep brown eyes settled on him and narrowed.

Fletch repeated: "Did you kill Steve Peterman?"

With a hard stare, she said, "What's your name, buster?"

"Fletcher," he said. Magnanimously, he added, "You can call me Fletch, though. When you call me."

27

Other reporters *t'ched* and shook their heads and otherwise expressed embarrassment at their crass colleague.

After staring at him a moment, Moxie said, slowly, clearly into the cameras, "I did not kill Steve Peterman."

The other reporters resumed clucking sympathetic questions. *How long have you known Steve Peterman? Were you close?*

Loudly, Fletch asked: "Ms Mooney—were you and Steve Peterman lovers?"

When she looked at Fletch this time, there was revulsion in her face.

"No," she said. "Mister Peterman and I were not lovers."

"What were your relations with Peterman?" Fletch asked.

Moxie hesitated, just slightly. "Strictly business. Steve was my manager," she said. "He took care of my business affairs. He helped produce this film." Her eyes closed fully and she took a deep breath. "And he was my friend."

Fletch thought he was doing a sufficiently surreptitious job of fading back through the crowd when he felt a hand on his arm.

He turned.

The short man was squinting at Fletch. He removed his hand.

"Haven't seen you before," he said. "Who are you?"

"I.M. Fletcher. Global Cable News."

"City guy, huh? National news type."

"You got it in one."

Behind the short man, the question rang out: *Do you think the murder of Peterman had anything to do with the earlier hit-and-run incident?*

Fletch couldn't hear Moxie's answer.

"Listen to me, Mister," the short reporter said. "We don't treat people like that around here."

"Like what?"

"That little lady—" The reporter jerked his tape recorder toward the sweat-stained shirt of another reporter. "—just lost her friend to death. Do you understand that? Asking her questions like you just did is just plain uncivil."

"Where you from?" Fletch asked. *"The Girl Scout Monthly?"*

"St. Petersburg."

"Listen, man—"

"Don't you 'listen, man' me." The short man pressed his index finger against Fletch's chest. "You get away from Ms Mooney and you get away from this story, or you'll find yourself stomped."

Fletch heard a reporter ask: *Ms Mooney, do you believe there are people trying to stop this film from being made?*

Again, Fletch did not hear her answer.

To the short reporter he said, "That would be uncivil of you."

"Don't you scoff at us, Mister. You work South and you mind your manners—you hear?"

"In this business," Fletch said to the short reporter, "there is no such thing as a wrong question. There are only wrong answers."

As he was leaving the lobby, Fletch heard a

reporter ask: *Ms Mooney, have you yourself received any death threats?*

"Hey," Moxie said.

She got into the front seat of the white Lincoln Continental and closed the door.

"Hey." Fletch was waiting in the back seat. She had taken exactly as long with the press as he thought she would. Without air-conditioning running, the car was hot, even on a gray day.

"Why are you sitting in the front seat?" Fletch asked.

"I'm a democratic star."

A few people were milling around the car, looking in.

"You believe in Equity?"

"And Equity believes in me. I pay my dues."

She sat sideways on the front seat and put her tanned arm along the top of the backrest.

"I may call you Fletch?"

"When you call me."

"That's a funny name. Think of all the things with which it rhymes."

"Yes," he mused. "Canelloni, for one. Prognathous, lasket, checkerberry, scantling, Pyeshkov, modulas, Gog and Magog."

"You know any other big words?"

"That's it."

"Thanks for what you did for me in there." Moxie smiled. "Pulling the teeth of the other reporters—and all those to come."

"Thought there was a need for one or two clear, simple statements on the incident from you."

"Didn't I do well?"

"You did. Of course."

"'Steve Peterman was my friend'." Moxie sort-of quoted, with a sort-of choke in her throat. "The bastard. I could have killed him."

"Someone agreed with you, apparently." Outside the window nearest Fletch stood a heavy woman in a gaily printed dress. "Moxie, they have to have this murder solved in a matter of hours."

"Why?" Her face was as free of wrinkles as if she had never read a book. Moxie had read books. "Why do you say that?"

"Steve wasn't shot. Like from a distance. He was stabbed. In public."

"Steve was just dying to get on *The Dan Buckley Show*," she drawled.

"There were cameras all over the place. There were cameras working the talk show. Local press were everywhere taking pictures of everything and everybody that had paint on it, whether it moved or not."

"Rather daring of whoever did it."

"And security was so tight on location they have the names and reason for being there of everyone within yodeling distance."

"Good," Moxie said. "Let's consider the damned thing solved."

"Are you sure this isn't one of Peterman's grand publicity schemes gone awry? Like the knife was just supposed to land on the stage, or something?"

"You're kidding. Steve wouldn't risk getting a spot on his slacks if he saw an orphanage on fire."

"Hey," Fletch said.

"What?"

"Stop acting tough."

She read his face. "What am I doing, protecting myself?"

"I would say so," he answered. "It's not every day the guy sitting next to you gets stabbed. A person you know, someone important to you."

"I guess so." She sighed. "I was having real problems with Steve, Fletch. Which is why I asked you to come down. I wanted to talk it out with somebody. I was finding it very difficult to be nice to him."

"Not being nice is not the same as being murderous."

"What?"

"Forget it. You're fighting shock, Moxie. Makin' like a heartless vamp."

"Yeah."

"You know it?"

"I guess so. Sure."

"You and Steve were close at one time."

"Steve was just using me," she said quietly. "Where's Marge? Is she okay?"

Fletch shrugged. "I expect she's being taken care of."

"They questioned her first," Moxie said. "In a car. At the beach."

"I see. Were Steve and Marge close?"

"I wouldn't say Steve was close to anybody but his banker."

"I was thinking of Marge," Fletch said.

"Good," Moxie said. "Steve never thought of her."

Her head was down and she was speaking softly. Beneath her tan, her skin had whitened. The enormity of what had happened was finally sinking into her. "Phew," she said. "I guess I am confused. I'm so used to people dying on stage and on camera with me. You know? Of acting out my reaction."

"I know."

"Steve is really dead?" She had turned her face from him. "Steve is really dead."

He flicked his tongue against the side of her neck. "Hang in there, Moxie." He opened the car door to get out. "I'll pick you up for dinner. Eight o'clock okay?"

"At La Playa," she said.

He had one foot on the pavement.

She cork-screwed around on the front seat. "Fletch?"

"Yeah?" He put his head back inside the car. Her cheeks were wet with tears.

"Find Freddy for me, will you?"

"Freddy? Is he here?"

"Oh, yes."

"Oh, God."

"He's playing the attentive father these days to me, or retired on me, or something."

"Let me guess which."

"He shouldn't be loose in public, with all this goin' on. The murder."

"Is he boozin'?"

"You need to ask?"

There was sand on the rear rug of the Lincoln.

Moxie said, "I suspect all that little squiggles in his brain have finally turned their toes up in the booze. Can't blame 'em. They've been drownin' in booze for years."

Over the car's blue rug, perfect images flashed for Fletch: Frederick Mooney on stage as Willy Loman, Richard III, and Lear. On film as Falstaff, as Disraeli, as Captain Bligh, as a baggy-pants comic, as a decent Montana rancher turned decent politician, as Scanlon on Death Row, as...

"He was the best," Fletch said, "even when he was stinko."

"History," Moxie said.

"Where should I look?"

"One of the joints on Bonita Beach. He drove up with us this morning. Freddy never wanders far, when there's a handy bar."

Fletch chuckled. "The thought of Freddy makes poets of us all."

"See you at eight," she said. "Thanks, Fletch."

"Okay."

Walking back toward the police station, Fletch noticed big, blowsy, wet clouds blowing in from the northwest.

5

"Okay," Fletch said to the secretary sitting at the desk between the doors marked INVESTIGA-TIONS and CHIEF OF POLICE, "I'll see whoev-er's in charge now."

The woman in the light yellow blouse looked at him as if he had just fallen from the moon. The lobby was still full of people.

"Have you been called?" asked the woman who had been doing the calling.

"No," Fletch said, "but I'm willing to serve."

The Investigations door opened and Dan Buckley came out looking as if he had been tumble-dried. The reporters rose to him like a puff of soot. Even without smiling, there was still amiable assurance on Buckley's face.

The short reporter glared at Fletch and made a point of stepping into the space between him and Buckley.

Are you going to run the tape of this show on television?

"No, no," Buckley answered. "I'm turning every centimeter of tape over to the police. The police will have our complete cooperation. Such a tragedy."

A middle-aged woman with handsomely waved brown hair came through the door marked IN-VESTIGATIONS. Fletch had never seen a police shirt so well filled. Her badge lay comfortably on her left breast. She had typewritten sheets in her hand. She was about to say something to the secretary.

"I'm next," Fletch informed her.

She, too, looked at Fletch as if he had just arrived from the moon.

"Fletcher," he said.

She looked down her list, turned a page, looked down the list, turned another page, looked down the list. "Honey," she said, "you're last."

Fletch grinned. "I bet you've been wanting to come to the end of that list."

She grinned back at him, waved the typewritten sheets at him, and said, "Come on in."

Going behind her desk, she said, "I'm Chief of Detectives Roz Nachman."

Fletch closed the door behind him.

Sitting down at her desk she peered into the window of her audio-recorder to see how much tape was left.

"Sit down, sit down," she said.

He did.

"Why don't I just give you a statement," he said. "Save time. Save you the bother of asking a lot of questions."

She shrugged. "Go ahead." She pushed the Record button on her tape machine.

"Name's I. M. Fletcher."

Sitting behind her desk, hands folded in her lap, Chief of Detectives Roz Nachman looked at Fletch's moccasins, his legs, his shorts, his tennis shirt, his arms, his neck, his face. Her smile was tolerant: that of someone about to hear a tale about fairies and witches.

"I arrived at the shooting location of the film *Midsummer Night's Madness* on Bonita Beach at about five minutes past three this afternoon. At the security gate, I showed my press credentials from Global Cable News. The security guard told me that the taping would continue until shortly before four. He directed me to the pavillion where a bar had been set up. He said a reception for the television crew and press was planned for after the taping.

"I went directly to the pavillion. Only one other person was present in the pavillion all the time I was there, a woman who later identified herself to me as the wife of the deceased. Marge Peterman. She was watching, on a television monitor, the taping of the show. I could see, at a distance and not clearly, the actual set of *The Dan Buckley Show.* I could also see, but not clearly, the monitor screen. In fact, I was looking at neither. I poured myself a glass of orange juice from the bar. My attention was called to the incident by Marge Peterman's saying, 'What happened to Steve?'.

"I looked across at the set and saw that Peterman was sitting in an odd position. I stood behind Mrs Peterman to get a better view of the monitor. On the monitor I saw blood dribbling from Peterman's mouth. This was at three twenty-three.

"I helped Mrs Peterman away from the pavillion, sat her in a chair at the side of the parking lot, got her some coffee, and sat with her alone until three fifty-three when some other people, Dan Buckley among them, came along, broke the news to her, and took charge of her.

"End of statement."

"You are a reporter," Roz Nachman mused. "Concise. To the point. What you could see, what you did see. Exact times by your watch. You didn't mention the ghost you saw pass through the talk-show set and drive a knife into Peterman's back."

"What?"

"Now, Mister Fletcher, despite your very complete and, I'm sure, very accurate statement, will you permit some questions?"

"Sure."

"Good of you. You're sure of the exact time?"

"I'm a reporter. Something happens, I look at my watch."

"Why were you on location of this filming?"

"To see Moxie Mooney."

"On assignment?"

"These days I get to make up my own assignments."

"From your appearance I would have taken you for something less than a managing editor."

"Didn't you know?" Fletch said. "Everyone is something less than a managing editor—star athletes, heads of state, reporters, chiefs of detectives—"

"You said no one else was in the pavillion except you and Mrs Peterman. Not even a bartender?"

"No. We were alone."

"Did Mrs Peterman know you were there?"

"I don't think so. I wasn't wearing shoes. I had been told to be quiet during the taping. She was engrossed in watching the monitor..."

"If she didn't know you were there, to whom was she speaking when she said, 'What happened to Steve?' or whatever it was she said?"

"She said, 'What happened to Steve?'," Fletch said, firmly.

"Sorry. I'm used to dealing with less, uh, professional witnesses."

"I think Mrs Peterman was talking to herself. From her tone of voice I would say she was frightened, alarmed. Which is why I moved over behind her, to see what she was seeing."

"Had you ever seen Marjory Peterman before?"

"No."

"During the time you took her away from the pavillion, got her coffee, sat with her, what did she say?"

"Nothing, really. Just little things, like 'What's taking so long?', 'Why doesn't someone come and tell me what happened?' Oh, yeah, she said she wanted to go in the ambulance with Steve."

"So she knew her husband had been wounded, shall we say?"

Fletch hesitated. "She may have known in her heart her husband was dead. He certainly looked dead on the monitor."

"Did she say anything to indicate she knew her husband had been dealt with violently? Murdered?"

Fletch thought. "No. I don't think she said anything more than I've told you."

"'Don't think'?"

"I know. I know she didn't say anything more." On the foot of the leg crossed over his knee, the moccasin was half off. "Except to identify herself to me as Marge Peterman."

"In response to a question?"

"I had asked her if she was Peterman's wife."

"You saw roughly the same thing Marjory Peterman saw, Mister Fletcher. What did you think had happened to Peterman?"

"I was trying to think what could have happened to him. I guess I was thinking he had suffered some kind of an internal hemorrhage. To account for the blood on his lips."

"You did not consider the possibility of murder?"

"No way. The son of a bitch was on television. I hadn't heard a gunshot. Who'd think of anyone sticking a knife into someone else on an open, daylit stage, with three cameras running?"

"That, Mister Fletcher," said Nachman looking down at her blotter, "is why I've called this meeting. So." She swiveled her chair sideways to the desk. "You had never seen Marjory Peterman before. But you did know Steven Peterman?"

"Ah." Fletch felt color come to his cheeks. "You say that because I called the son of a bitch a son of a bitch."

"Yes," Nachman nodded. "I could characterize that as a clue of your having a previous, personal opinion of the deceased."

"I knew him slightly."

"How's that?" She turned her head and smiled at him. "I think it's time for another one of your concise statements, Mister Reporter."

"About nine months ago, he spent a longish weekend at my home in Italy. Cagna, Italy."

"Italy? Are you Italian?"

"I'm a citizen of the United States. Voting age, too."

"Is Italy where you got those shorts?"

Fletch looked down at his shorts and lifted the hands in his pockets. "They have good pockets. You can carry books in them, notebooks, sandwiches..."

"Or a knife," she said simply. "In most of the clothes these film people are wearing you couldn't conceal a vulgar thought. So. Are you going to tell me why Peterman visited you in Italy?"

"Of course."

"Tell me first why you have a house in Italy. I mean, a struggling young reporter, no matter how precise you are...Cagna's on the Italian Riviera, isn't it?"

"I have a little extra money."

"Must be nice to be born rich."

"Must be," Fletch said. "I wasn't."

She waited for a further explanation, but Fletch offered none.

"Now, I'd like to know why Peterman visited you at your Italian palace."

"He was travelling with Moxie Mooney. She was on a press tour of Europe. Moxie visited me. At my little villa. He was with her."

Her eyebrows rose. "So? You knew Moxie Mooney before?"

"I've always known Moxie Mooney. We were in school together."

"Some humble reporter," Nachman commented. "Entertain big movie stars and film producers at his Italian estate. Wait until I tell the guys and gals on the local police beat. They can't even afford to go to the movies twice a week. You must spell better than they do."

"Never mind," Fletch said. "They don't like me already."

"So on that weekend at your 'little villa' in Italy, who slept with whom?"

"What a question."

"Yes," Nachman said. "It's a question. Were Moxie Mooney and Steven Peterman intimate?"

"No."

"You're making me ask every question, aren't you?"

"Yes."

"Were you and Ms Mooney intimate?"

"Sure."

"Why 'sure'? Are you and Ms Mooney lovers?"

"Off and on."

"'Off and on'." Chin on hand, elbow on desk

blotter, Roz Nachman contemplated what *off and on* could mean. Finally, she shook her head. "I think you should explain."

"Not sure I can."

"Try," she said. "So the hems of Justice will be neat."

"You see." Fletch looked at the ceiling. "Each time Moxie and I meet, here and there, now and then, we pretend we've never met before. We pretend we're just meeting for the first time."

Roz frowned. "No. I don't really see."

"Okay."

"Would you walk that past me again?"

"It's simple." Fletch took another long look at the ceiling. "We've known each other a long time and well. I suppose we love each other. So each time we meet, we pretend we've never met before. Which is true, you see. We never really have met before. Because people today aren't really the same people they were yesterday or the day before. Every day you're a new person; you have new thoughts, new experiences. You should never meet a person and presume she's the same person she was last week. Because she's not. It's just the reality of existence."

"I see," Roz Nachman said, staring at him. "And *then* you jump into bed together?"

"Shucks." Fletch lowered his eyelids.

"If you two have so much fun together, why don't you stay together?"

"Oh, no." Fletch glanced at the tape recorder. "You see, we probably can't stand each other. I mean, in reality."

"Because you're both much too beautiful," Roz Nachman said. "Physically."

"No, no," Fletch said. "Moxie's the most beautiful crittur who's ever eaten a french fry."

"Has she ever eaten a french fry?"

"One or two. When she can get 'em."

"She doesn't look like she's ever eaten a french fry."

"It's more complex than all that. Maybe it's that we both play the same kind of games. We make a poor audience for each other."

"'Games'." Nachman had picked up a pencil and was running its point loosely back and forth over a piece of paper. "I wonder what that means."

"Why do I feel like I'm sitting in the office of a public school Guidance Counselor?"

"The statement you gave when you first came in here, Mister Fletcher, was factually accurate." Nachman waved her pencil at the tape recorder. "And a complete lie."

"Me? Lie?"

"No wonder you're such a rich reporter you can live on the Italian Riviera."

"I know I flunked Mechanical Drawing, Ms Frobisher," Fletch said, "but I really want to take Auto Repair a second year."

"You certainly gave the impression you came to Bonita Beach as a reporter to interview Ms Mooney. You certainly did not volunteer the information that you knew the murder victim, or Ms Mooney— the latter intimately. Is all this part of some game you're playing?"

"All the information you've elicited from me is irrelevent. I didn't kill anybody."

"I wonder if you'd mind leaving that decision to the authorities?"

"I sure would mind. All I'm saying is that Marge Peterman didn't kill him either. I was with her at the moment Peterman was being murdered."

"The truth, Mister Fletcher, is that no one I've talked with so far on this list testifies to having seen either you or Marge Peterman from shortly after three until shortly before four."

"What are you saying?"

"And I've never known a reporter who can afford a house of any kind on the Italian Riviera."

Fletch said, "I write good."

"Was Ms Mooney expecting you today?"

"Yes."

"And what kind of a game is she playing?"

"She's not playing any kind of a game. You're turning two-penny psychoanalysis into—"

"Let's go on." Sitting straight at her desk, Nachman referred to some handwritten notes.

"At least I'm answering your questions."

Nachman glared at him. "You know what happens to you if you don't."

"Yeah," said Fletch. "I don't get to take Auto Repair next semester."

"What was your impression of Steven Peterman when he spent the weekend at your house in Italy?"

"You're asking for an opinion."

"Something tells me you have one."

"I do."

"What is it?"

"He was a son of a bitch."

"Why do you say that?"

"Because you asked me."

"Why do you characterize Steven Peterman as 'a son of a bitch'?"

"He was a nuisance. Look," Fletch said, "the house there is on the beach. Above the beach. It's a beach house."

"You're loosing your conciseness."

"People hang around in swim suits. Pasta and fish for supper on the patio. A little wine. Music."

"You're saying Peterman didn't fit in."

"Always in a three-piece suit. He wore a cravat. Wouldn't go on the beach because he didn't want sand against his Gucci loafers."

"Intolerable behavior."

"Always on the telephone. Calling Rome, Geneva, Paris, London, New York, Los Angeles, Buenos Aires. I know. I got the phone bill. It would have been cheaper to have had the entire French government for the weekend."

"All right. He was an inconsiderate houseguest."

"Every night he insisted everybody get dressed up and plod through the most expensive cafes, restaurants, night clubs, casinos on the Riviera."

"And you paid?"

"Everytime a bill came, he was on the telephone somewhere."

"Okay."

"Worse. Everytime he saw Moxie, he bothered her with some clause of some contract, or some detail of her schedule, ran over the names of people she was to meet in Berlin two weeks from then, Brussels, who, what, where, when, why. He never left her alone. She was there to relax."

"And play games with you. You two avoided him?"

"As much as we could. It's hard to ignore a government-in-residence."

"You played hide-and-seek with him."

"Yeah."

"Marjory Peterman was not with you that weekend. Right?"

"Right."

"Where was she?"

Fletch shrugged. "Home milking her minks, for all I know."

"I repeat the question: you have never seen or spoken with Marjory Peterman before today?"

"Right. No. Never."

"You knew the victim, Steven Peterman, and admit not liking him."

"I would never murder anyone over a phone bill. Instead, I just wouldn't pay it. I'd move to Spain."

"And you have this complicated love-slash-hate relationship with Moxie Mooney."

Fletch looked at her from under lowered eyelids. "Don't make too much of that."

She looked evenly back at him. "Frankly, Mister Fletcher, I think you and Ms Mooney are capable of anything...together." She glanced at the tape recorder, at Fletch, and at the typewritten list on

47

her desk. "Okay, Mister Fletcher. I guess I don't need to tell you not to leave the Fort Myers area."

"You don't need to tell me."

Roz Nachman turned off the tape recorder.

6

Soaking wet from running through the heavy rain, Fletch slowed at the top of the outside, sheltered stairs when he recognized Frederick Mooney's famous profile.

His back to the white, churning Gulf of Mexico, Mooney was sitting alone at a long table on the second floor verandah of a drinks-and-eat place on Bonita Beach. On the table in front of him was a half empty litre bottle. In his hand was a half empty glass.

Fletch ambled to the bar. "Beer," he said.

"Don't care which kind?" The bartender had the tight, permanently harrassed look of the retired military.

"Yeah," Fletch said. "Cold."

The bartender put a can of cold beer on the bar. "Some rain," he said.

"Enough." Fletch popped the lid on the beer can. "Mister Mooney been here long?"

No one else was on the verandah.

"You come to collect him?"

"Yeah."

"Couple of hours."

"Has he had much to drink?"

"I don't know."

Fletch swallowed some beer. "You don't know?"

"Drinks out of his own bottle. Carries it with him. Five Star Fundador Cognac. I don't keep such stuff."

At Frederick Mooney's feet was an airlines travel bag.

"You allow that?"

"No. But he tips well. As long as he pays a big rent for the glass, I don't care. After all, he is Frederick Mooney."

There was a roll of thunder from the northwest. Rain was blowing into the verandah.

"Does he come here every day?"

"No. I think he hits all the places on the beach."

"In what kind of shape was he when you rented him the glass?"

"He'd been drinkin' somewhere else before. Took him ten minutes to get up the stairs. Heard him comin'. Had to help him sit down and then bring his bag over to him."

The rain spray was passing over Mooney.

"Think of a famous, talented man like that..."

The bartender popped a can of beer for himself. "You an actor, too?"

"Yeah," said Fletch. "At this moment."

"I mean, you've come from the film crew, and all, to pick him up. What films you ever been in?"

"*Song of The South*," Fletch said. "You ever see it?"

"That the one with Elizabeth Taylor?"

"No," said Fletch. "Maud Adams."

"Oh, yeah. I remember."

"He ever talk to anybody?" Fletch asked, nodding to Mooney.

"Oh, yeah, he's friendly. He talks to everybody. Usually the old ladies are six deep around him. Young people, too. Mostly he recites lines. Sometimes he gets loud."

"Good for business though, huh?"

"Sure."

"A traveling tourist attraction."

"You'd think he'd be livin' on the Riviera, or something. Superstar like that. He's a lonely man."

"All the wrong people live on the Riviera."

Fletch walked over and stood at the edge of Mooney's table.

Mooney did not look up.

Lightning flashed in the north sky.

"Your daughter sent me for you, Mister Mooney."

Mooney still did not look up. He was breathing rapidly, shallowly. Spray was lightly in his hair and on his shirt.

Suddenly, the great voice came out of this hunched over man, not loud, but with the compelling vibrato of an awfully good cello played by an awfully good musician.

"No, no, no, no." He looked up at Fletch. He spoke companionably. *"Come, let's away to prison. We two alone will sing like birds i' the cage. When thou dost ask me blessing, I'll kneel down, and ask of thee forgiveness."*

Fletch sat across from him at the empty table.

"So we'll live, and pray, and sing, and tell old tales, and laugh at gilded butterflies, and hear poor rogues talk of court news; and we'll talk with them, too: who loses and who wins, who's in, who's out; and take upon's the mystery of things, as if we were God's spies; and we'll wear out, in a wall'd prison, packs and sects of great ones that ebb and flow by the moon."

Mooney, palm outward, passed his hand between the stormy sky and his face, turning his head as he did so, finally fixing Fletch with a mad stare. Mooney looked utterly insane.

"Jeez."

Terror, horror had skittered up Fletch's spine. He gulped beer and took a breath.

"Actually..." Fletch cleared his throat. To his own ears his voice sounded like a flute played in a tin box. "I saw you in *King Lear* once. As an undergraduate. In Chicago. Not so long ago."

Mooney's face turned puckish. "Only once?" he asked.

"Only once. I had to sell my portable radio to afford that once."

"Lear," said Mooney. "The role Charles Lamb said could not be acted."

Fletch raised his beer can. "Nuts to Charles Lamb."

The hand that reached for the glass of cognac shook badly. "Nuts to Charles Lamb."

They drank.

"Do you act?" Mooney asked.

"No."

"What?" Mooney asked. "Not even badly?"

"There's been some trouble," Fletch said slowly, carefully. "On location. Someone's been stabbed."

Mooney's eyes were half-closed. Again his breath was coming in short, shallow strokes.

"There's been a murder," Fletch said.

Mooney sat back. He looked around, at the bar, at the verandah's roof, at the storm outside. His eyes were huge, with huge pupils, dark brown and wide set. Together they were the tragi-comic masks, each capable of holding a different expression simultaneously, one sombre, sad, emotional, the other, objective, thinking. Looking at him closely, Fletch wondered if one eye might actually be lower in the man's head than the other. He wondered if it was an actor's trick or an accident of birth. He wondered if it was an expression of the man's personality.

Mooney said, *"Do not abuse me."*

"Did you hear me? There's been a murder."

"I gather Marilyn is all right."

"Marilyn? Yes. She's okay. But she was sitting next to the victim when he was stabbed."

"And who was the victim?"

"Steven Peterman."

53

Mooney frowned. He scratched his gray, grizzly hair.

"Your daughter's manager, producer, whatever."

Mooney nodded.

"They were taping *The Dan Buckley Show*. In the middle of *Midsummer Night's Madness* location."

"Not a play within a play," commented Mooney, "but a stage within a stage."

"Within a stage," added Fletch. "Because the press was there, too, taking videotapes and still photographs."

"And no live audience."

"Not much of a one."

"How removed our art has become. No longer do we perform for the groundlings. For human beings we must distract from playing blackjacks in the dirt. No longer for the Dress Circle or The Balcony. But for banks and banks of cameras." Mooney leaned forward, picked up his glass and chuckled. "For the banks. Peterkin?"

"Peterman. Steven Peterman."

"Peterman was *in camera*." Mooney drained his glass. His eyes glazed. They crossed, slightly. He reached for the bottle with a very shakey hand. "Do you know the expression?"

"The thing is, Moxie's waiting for us."

"We'll just have a drink together, you and I. Talk of who's in and who's out. Get yourself a drink."

"I have one."

Mooney's eyes narrowed to find Fletch's beer can. "So you have."

He had poured himself a good three ounces.

"So who was this Peterperson. Much of a loss to the world, do you think?"

Fletch shrugged. "Moxie's manager. A producer of the film."

"And how did he die?"

"He got stabbed in the back."

Mooney laughed. "Typical of the business. The *hindustry*, as it's now called."

"I'm afraid your daughter is one of the prime suspects."

"Marilyn?"

"Yes."

"I wouldn't put it past her." Mooney looked speculatively over the railing through the storm, not seeing it.

Fletch hesitated. For such a genius, how drunk was drunk; was he seeing lucidity or Lear; was the subject Regan or Moxie? "You wouldn't put what past whom?"

"Murder." Mooney's eyes came back to Fletch. "Past Marilyn."

A worse shiver went down Fletch's spine, and up again where it hit the back of his head like a fistful of feathers.

Mooney lowered his eyes to the scarred table. "She's done it before."

"Done what?" Fletch blurted.

Mooney dug into a scar on the table with his thumb nail. "Murder," he said.

The surf pounded three times on the beach before Fletch had enough easy breath to say, "What are you talking about?"

"That incident at the school," Mooney said. "When

Marilyn was thirteen, fourteen. The year her benign Daddy—yours truly—decided to transfer her to a school in England at mid-term. November, I think it was. No one is supposed to know what precipitated the sudden transfer, of course. I said I wanted her near me. I was scarcely in England at all that year."

Fletch said, "I knew she spent a year or two in school in England."

"But you don't know why." Mooney then used the tired voice of someone reciting sad, ancient history. "At the private boarding school she was attending in California, her drama coach...maybe I could remember his name..." He gulped some of his drink. "...Can't. No matter. Little creep. Was found drowned at the edge of the school pond, his feet sticking out. Someone had bopped him on the head with a rock. Knocked unconscious. School authorities investigated. There were only three girls anywhere near the pond that afternoon. Marilyn was the closest. Marilyn was the only one of the three who knew the creep, was a student of his. Marilyn was the pitcher on the school's ballteam, entirely capable of forcefully beaning someone with a rock." Mooney hiccoughed. Then he sighed. "She did not like that drama coach. She had written me so—in flaming red pose. I mean, prose."

"The man could have slipped..."

"He was face down in the water. He had been hit on the back of the head. Murder most foul...and deliberate. Couldn't prove for a certainty who did it...that Marilyn did it. She was questioned. Good actress even then. Had her old man's blood, you know. Born with it. Veins are stuffed with it."

"So you hustled her to a school in England."

"Yes," Mooney said slowly. "She was being questioned, questioned, questioned. Don't object to questions, mind you. One or two of the answers might have been..." Mooney's voice went up the long trail.

"But if she was guilty of murder—"

Mooney jerked to attention. "She'd still be my daughter, damn it. Brilliant future. All that blood in her veins. Talent shouldn't be wasted." His shoulders eased into a more relaxed posture. "I think of the incident as nothing more than Ulysses bashing in his teacher's head with a lyre. There comes a time when one must do away with one's teacher, one way or another. Granted, Ulysses and Marilyn took a more dramatic approach than others..."

Fletch said, "She was having some trouble with Peterman. Which is why she asked me to come down to see her."

"What?" Mooney asked crisply. "You mean you're not in the *hindustry* at all?"

"No. I'm a reporter."

"Oops. Must mind my manners. Am I being interviewed?"

"No. You're not."

"I'm offended. Why not?"

"Because, sir, you're drunk."

"In your opinion..." Mooney paused. He blinked slowly. "...I'm drunk?"

"No offense."

"I'm always drunk," Mooney said. "No offense. It's my way of life. My being drunk has never stopped my giving a good interview. Or performance."

"I once read that you'd said you've made as many as thirty films dead drunk and don't remember anything about any of them. Is that true?"

Mooney's head seemed loose. Then he nodded sharply. "Tha's true."

"How can such a thing be true?"

"I love to see movies I know nothing about. Especially when I'm in them."

"I don't get it. How can you get yourself up for a scene, appear not drunk on the screen, when you're drunk?"

"Unreality," Mooney said. "Reality. The distortion of reality. You see?" he asked.

"No."

"I made a whole film, once, in Ankara. A year later, I told a reporter I'd never been in Turkey. Widely quoted. The studio said I'd been misquoted. That I'd said I had never been in a turkey." Mooney laughed. "I've been in turkeys. I guess I've also been in Turkey. Nice place, Turkey. I live in a nice place, in my mind. Filming's easy. It only takes a few minutes a day. I can always get myself up for it."

"Always?"

The pupils of Mooney's eyes were shaking, or glimmering with challenge. "Want to see me get myself up right now?"

Fletch said, "I think I just saw you do it. You were just Lear, in front of my eyes."

"I was? I did? I'll do it again." Mooney composed his face. He took a slow, deep breath. Behind his face something was pulling him to sleep. "I don't feel like it," he said.

He took a drink.

"Sorry, sir," Fletch said. "Don't mean to badger you. Just stupid curiosity, on my part."

"'S all right," Mooney said cheerily. "I'm used to being an object of ururosity. Cure-urosity."

"You're a great man."

"Like any other," said Mooney.

"Shall we go to the car? It's not raining so hard now."

"The car!" exclaimed Mooney. He looked around himself, then out at the beach. "What, have they stopped shooting for the day. Lose their light?"

"We've been sitting through a hell of a storm. Pouring rain. Thunder. Lightning."

Mooney looked confused, curious. He said, "I thought that was in *King Lear*."

"Come on." Fletch stood up. "Your daughter's waiting."

"Involved in a murder..."

"Something like that."

"I wonder...if she has a black veil in her wardrobe."

"I don't know," Fletch said. "Time to go."

"That bottle..." Mooney pointed at it. "...goes in that bag." He pointed at the wrong spot on the floor, to his right rather than his left, to where the airlines bag wasn't.

Fletch capped the bottle and put it in the bag.

There were three other full bottles in the bag, one empty, and some bulky odd rags.

Mooney swallowed the rest of his drink, stood up and lurched.

Fletch grabbed his arm.

"Going now?" the bartender asked.

"Thank you, Innkeeper," Mooney said, "for your superb horse."

"'Night, Mister Mooney."

"Horsepitality."

Fletch said, *"Will't please your highness walk?"*

Bent over, clutching Fletch's arm, Mooney grinned up at him. *"You must bear with me. Pray you now, forget and forgive. I am old and foolish."*

Getting him down the stairs was a chore. It took almost ten minutes.

When Mooney stepped out from under the roof he looked at the day, at the Gulf, at the rain as if he'd never seen it all before.

"Wet day," he said. "Think I'll go back to the hotel and slip into a dry martini."

"Think I'll go back to the hotel," Fletch said, "and slip into your daughter."

Mooney did not look at Fletch or turn his head but the skin just forward of his ear turned red.

Fletch put him in the back seat of the rented car.

On the drive to Vanderbilt Beach, Frederick Mooney took two swigs from his bottle and fell asleep. He snored loudly enough to awake anyone dozing in any balcony, anywhere.

7

"May I help you, sir?"

Through the glass of the front door of Hotel La Playa, the red jacketed bellman had seen Fletch drive up, get out of the car, and hesitate. It was after dark and Fletch was shoeless, in wet shorts and shirt.

"Yeah. Will you please tell Ms Mooney her father and driver are waiting for her?"

"Certainly, sir."

Fletch leaned against the wet car. Even with doors and windows closed he could hear Frederick Mooney snoring in the back seat.

Within five minutes Moxie came through the door and down the steps.

She was wearing a simple, short, black dress. And a black veil.

Fletch held the passenger seat's door open for her and got in the driver's side.

In the back seat Frederick Mooney turned quiet.

"My God," Moxie expostulated. "What's the world coming to? Think of a man like Steve Peterman being stabbed to death right before my very eyes!"

"Was it?"

"Beg pardon, young man?"

Fletch headed the car back to Route 41. "Was it before your very eyes?"

"No. Really, I didn't see a thing. I don't see how such a thing could have happened."

"Were you close?"

"Like brother and sister. Steve's been with me years. Helping me. Through thick and thin. Through good times and bad times. Ups and downs."

"Coming and going."

"Coming and going."

"Arrivals and departures."

"Arrivals and departures."

From the back seat, Frederick Mooney said, "Very good, girlie."

Moxie pulled off her hat and veil and threw them on the backseat next to her father. She was grinning. "Thought you'd like it, O.L."

"I understand if you don't carry off this performance very well indeed, darling daughter, your next engagement might be a long one in the cooler."

"He's doing the role of Scanlon," Moxie explained to Fletch.

"Oh."

"The Saint on Murderers' Row."

"I see."

"Was it you what busted the creep's plumbing, daughter?"

"I didn't mean to, honest, I didn't. See I was parin' my nails with this shiv when he come along real careless like and backed into me." Moxie shook her head. "Real careless."

"From what Peterman tells me," Mooney said, "this is a serious matter."

In the front seat, Fletch and Moxie looked at each other in sincere wonderment.

"Peterman?" Moxie asked.

Through the rear view mirror Fletch saw Mooney indicate he meant Fletch.

"Peterman," Mooney said.

"O.L." Moxie exhaled. "This man's name is Fletcher. Peterman is the name of the man what got punctured."

Mooney muttered, "I thought he said his name was Peterman."

"Dear O.L.," Moxie commented. "Always very up on my affairs. Makes a point of knowing everyone in my life. A friend to all my friends. All in all, a doting father."

"So which one got stabbed?" Mooney asked.

Fletch said, "The other one."

"Then you're Peterman," Mooney asserted.

"No," said Fletch. "I'm Fletcher. I'm the one who told you about Peterman."

"It doesn't make any difference," concluded Mooney after a pull on his bottle. "It's a very serious matter."

After a moment, seeing Mooney's head nod in the rearview mirror, Fletch asked Moxie, "You call your father O.L.?"

"Only to his face."

"I never heard that. You've always called him Freddy."

"Originally it was O.L.O. Short for Oh, Luminous One. My mother started calling him that when they were first married, young, starting out. Still does. When her poor confused mind churns out anything at all. I visited her last month. At the home. Poor mama. Anyway, over the years it got shortened to O.L."

"They call me Oh, Hell," Mooney announced from the back seat, his voice resonating in the closed car. "For short, they call me Oh, Heck." He tipped the bottle up to his mouth.

Moxie looked through the rain spotted window. They had turned north on Route 41. "Where we going?"

"Dinner."

"And what do we do with the superstar in the back seat?"

"Take him with us."

"You've never seen Freddy in a restaurant."

"No."

"People gasp and fall off their chairs. They send over drinks, competitively. They line up to shake his hand and have a few words with him, so he never gets anything to eat. They never seem to realize how drunk he already is. I call it the Public Campaign To Kill Frederick Mooney."

"He's still alive."

"Used to find it damned embarrassing, when I was small. Public Drunkenness Being Praised."

Mooney said, *"I should e'en die with pity to see another thus."*

"Oh, God," Moxie said. "Lear. What got him on Lear? Did I say something Regan-like?"

"I think it started when I first found him in the bar," Fletch said. "The first thing I said to him was something like *'your daughter sent me to fetch you'.*"

"Yes," Moxie said. "That would be enough of a cue to get him going on Lear. And did he recite to you?"

"Yes," Fletch said. "It was marvelous. In thunder and lightning and pelting rain."

Moxie reached back and patted Mooney on the knee. "That's O.K., O.L., I never missed a meal."

"Damned right you didn't," Mooney said.

"You put me in school and mama in the hospital but nobody ever missed a meal."

Mooney shook his head in agreement. "It's a damned serious matter. I told Fletcher that."

Moxie shook her head and turned around again just as they were passing a sign saying 41. "Damned Route 41. Came here to make a movie and it seems I've spent my whole time so far on Route 41. Going back and forth. Vanderbilt Beach to Bonita Beach. Bonita Beach to Vanderbilt Beach. Life's damned hard on a working girl."

"What's this about a hit-and-run accident?" Fletch asked.

"You know about that?"

"Heard a reporter ask you something about it."

"I don't think it's related," Moxie said. "I mean, to Steve's death. It was Geoffrey McKensie's wife."

"Why does that name seem familiar? Geoffrey McKensie?"

"Australian director." Moxie yawned. "A very good Australian director. Maybe the best director in the whole world. He's done three quiet pictures. Don't think any of them have been seen much outside Australia. I've screened all three. They're magnificent. He brings up character beautifully. Very sensitive. You know, he takes the time, the fraction of a second it takes, to permit a character to do something really revealing, maybe contradictory, uh... you know what I mean?"

"No."

"Oh. Well. I was really hoping he'd direct this *Midsummer Night's Madness*. I thought he was going to direct it. He came here to direct it."

"And he's not directing it."

"Sy Koller is directing. Who is a nice man, and good enough."

"You mean the man, this McKensie, came all the way from Australia thinking he had a job and didn't have one?"

"With wife."

"How can that happen?"

"Such things happen all the time in the industry. There's a magic hex word in this industry— the word *bankable*."

"You mean investible?"

66

"Digestible. In this business when the noncreative people have to make a decision and don't know how to make a decision based on creativity and talent they make the decision based on this word *bankable*. They argue that they can get bankers, investors interested in one property, or person, but not another. What it really comes down to is, *my property and friends are bankable, and your property and friends are not bankable*. You see?"

"And this Godfrey McKensie was declared not bankable?"

"Geoffrey McKensie. Yes."

"After he got here?"

"After he got here Sy Koller became available. Another film he was working on fell through."

"And Sy Koller is bankable?"

"Sy Koller's last five films have all been failures. Financially and critically. Disasters."

"And that makes him bankable?"

"Sure. Steve felt Sy was due to make a good picture."

"And this poor Aussie who's made three good pictures and has flown half way around the world to make a film is not bankable?"

"Right. Because nobody knows his name. Yet. Nobody here has seen his films. Everybody knows Sy Koller's name."

"They know him as a failed director. Pardon me for not believing a word of this."

"It is incredible. Which is why a person like me has a person like Steve Peterman to deal with all this. Who can understand it? Who wants to understand it!"

"Doesn't this man, McKensie, have any rights?"

"Sure. He has the right to sue. He probably is suing. But I don't think a film has been made since *Birth Of A Nation* without people suing. And people should have sued over that, if they didn't. Anyway, about ten days ago Geoffrey McKensie's wife got run over. On Old Route 41. She had stopped at a fruit and flower stand, bought some flowers and was recrossing the road to her car when she got hit. The driver didn't stop."

"Killed?"

"Died three hours later in the hospital."

"No witnesses?"

"Just the woman at the flower stand. She said the car that hit Mrs McKensie was going very fast. Was either blue or green. Driven by either a man or a woman. We're going rather far for dinner, aren't we? All the way into Fort Myers?"

"And McKensie is still around?"

"Sure."

"The funeral...I should think he'd want to go home..."

"First he had to bury his wife. Then I suppose he had to get lawyers. I hope he's suing. Maybe he has to be on location to make his suit good. I don't know. I like him. This is all terrible."

At a red light Fletch turned right.

"This is the airport," Moxie said.

"Yes, it is."

"We're eating at an airport?"

"More or less."

"We've gone out of our way to eat at an airport?"

Fletch didn't answer.

"Irwin Maurice Fletcher, I have spent enough

of my life confronted with the utterly indifferent, unappetizing food served at airports."

"Call me Oh, Wondrous One for short. Or, O-l-l."

"I'll never call you for dinner."

"Be fair. You've never had a good meal at an airport?"

"Never."

"Never ever?"

"Once."

"Where? Which airport?"

"Why should I tell you? Look what you're doing to me. Taking me to dinner at an airport!"

Fletch craned his head lower and looked up through the windshield. "Above an airport, actually."

"Great. Dinner in a Control Tower. Very relaxing."

"Weather's clearing, you see. Thought it might be nice to go up in an airplane, have a leisurely snack while we watch the moon rise."

"Serious?"

"Should time out just about right."

He pulled into a parking space.

She was staring across the front seat at him. "You've hired an airplane for dinner?"

He turned off the motor. "Where else can you two superstars go tonight? One of you has been drinking all day—"

"—all life—"

"—and the other one's as jittery as a talking doll in the hands of a small boy."

"Fletcher, you're something else."

"I know that. *What* else is the question."

He got out and opened the car's trunk. She followed him behind the car.

"What's that?" she asked.

"A picnic basket. Had it made up while I was looking for Freddy. Lots of goodies. Chopped ham and pickle. Shrimp. Champagne."

He took the hamper out and slammed the trunk's lid.

He opened a back door of the car. "Mister Mooney?"

He shook Mooney's arm. The bottle in Mooney's lap was almost empty.

"We're at the airport, sir." Mooney blinked at him. "Thought we'd get high for dinner, sir."

"Very thoughtful of you." Mooney began to climb out of the car. "Very thoughtful indeed, Mister Peterman."

8

"I don't see the moon," Moxie said.

"Complaints! Have to be patient." Fletch was pouring champagne into long-stemmed glasses. "A little bubbly, Mister Mooney?"

"Never touch the stuff," Mooney said. "Upsets my cognac."

They were sitting in large leather swivel chairs. Each had a safety belt strapped across the lap. The passenger section of the airplane was furnished and decorated partly as a living room, partly as an office.

At first, the pilot who had escorted them across the dark runway had watched worriedly Frederick Mooney's stumbling gait. It did not make him less worried that Frederick Mooney was singing, very loudly and very badly, *If I had the wings of an angel*...As they were passing under a light, the pilot's face did a double-look and expressed shock at recognizing Moxie Mooney. He looked sharply and recognized Frederick Mooney. Solicitiously, he helped Frederick Mooney up the steps and strapped him into the seat himself.

The plane took off immediately.

"I presume we're to fly in circles," Moxie said.

"How on earth can you fly any other way?" Fletch asked.

Seated, Fletch was setting the pull-out table within easy reach of their chairs with things from the picnic basket. He removed the protective cellophane from the plates of cut, assorted sandwiches. Opened the containers of iced shrimp, lobster tails, their sauces, salads. Dealt plates and cutlery and napkins around the table. Last out of the basket was a little white vase and a long-stemmed red rose. He poured champagne into the vase, put the rose in it, and set the rose in the middle of the table.

Watching him, Moxie said, "You would make an interesting husband, after all."

"I did," Fletch said. "Twice."

"As the lady said," intoned Frederick Mooney, with a cold look at his daughter, "just as they were leading her away, 'I was cursed by marriage to an interesting man'."

Fletch looked from one to another, then said, "Anyone for eats?"

Both Mooneys wordlessly heaped their plates with every food in sight. "Enough for the vanity of

72

film stars," Fletch muttered, helping himself from the remainders. "Good thing I bought for six."

Plate in lap, Mooney swiveled his chair to look out the window while he ate.

"Now," Fletch said to Moxie, after she had downed six quarter-sandwiches, four lobster tails and half her shrimp, "want to tell me why you asked me to come down here? Or have you had enough for today? Or maybe it isn't relevent any more...?"

"You're hard enough to find," grumbled Moxie. "It took me the better part of a week to trace you down."

"I was in Washington," Fletch said, "trying to find The Bureau of Indian Affairs."

"Did you find it?" She was chewing a lobster tail.

"I narrowed it down to one of three telephone booths."

She wiped her hands on a napkin. "I seem to be in real financial trouble."

"How is that possible?"

"You tell me."

"Some nights you're on two television channels simultaneously. You're on the cables so much I should think you'd twang. Your films play the theaters. Last Christmas you did the first one hundred days of *A Broadway Hit*—"

"And I'm drowning in debt. Explain that to me."

"I'd like to understand it myself. You're smudging the American dream. The rich-and-famous dream."

There were tears in her eyes. She ducked her head to her plate. "I work hard. I have to. So many people are counting on me. My work contributes to the income of literally thousands of people now. We've got my mother in this fabulously expensive sanatorium in Kansas. I've taken over some of the cost from Freddy." She lowered her voice. "And I don't have to be much of a fortune teller to say that pretty soon I'm going to have to take it all over. And everyone knows this is just a crazy business I'm in!" she said more loudly. "No security. Bankable today, a bum tomorrow. A person like me can't get so much out of herself if she thinks that next week, next month, next year sometime she's going to be on the sidewalk!"

"Have some shrimp."

"I have some shrimp."

"Have some more shrimp."

"I don't want any more shrimp," she said with annoyance. Then she looked at him. "Was that your Sympathetic Routine Number 12?"

"Number 9, actually. I wish you wouldn't see through me so quickly. It makes me blush."

"You've never blushed in your life."

"Why don't you try to tell me in some sort of narrative form, some sequence—"

"Can't."

"I'm just a simple journalist, temporarily out of work—"

"The whole thing landed on me like a big bomb just a couple of weeks ago. Just before I was due on location for *Midsummer Night's Madness*. Hell of a way to start a picture. Looking drawn and haggard."

"You've never looked drawn and haggard in your life." He looked at the lights in her tanned, blond skin, the lights in her blond hair. "Ashes and honey don't mix."

"Okay," she said. "The story. A couple of weeks ago, I get a call from a man at the Internal Revenue Service who says he's very sorry to bother me *but*..."

"With them it's the but that counts."

"Right away I told him to call Steve Peterman, that Steve Peterman takes care of all my business affairs, taxes, etcetera, etcetera. And he said that was why he was calling me personally because maybe Mister Peterman hadn't told me that if I didn't do something within a matter of days, I was going to jail. Me going to jail—not Steve Peterman."

"Oh, Moxie, the Internal Revenue Service always talks tough. I once had a very funny experience—"

"Right now, Fletch, I'm not interested in the comic side of the Internal Revenue Service. I asked the man what he was talking about. He said I had gone way beyond my last extension, and a lot of other things I didn't understand. I asked him to slow down and speak in a language I could understand."

"That's asking a bit too much of any government."

"Well, he did. He was really very kind. I sort of understood him, after a while. Instead of paying my taxes over the last years, Steve has been asking for extensions. So I'm years behind. I asked the man how much I owe. He said they don't know. They think it's a considerable whack of money. But then he said something or other about all the money I've had going in and out of the country makes things rather confusing."

"What money have you had going in and out of the country?"

"I have no idea."

"*Into* the country I understand, maybe. Being in the film business you probably have some foreign income. *Out of* the country I don't understand. Do you have any investments abroad?"

"Not that I know of. Why should I?"

"Well, it's possible Steve had you invested in French perfumery or something."

"He never mentioned it. You haven't heard the worst. I was greatly upset. I called Steve, and that made me more upset. He was distinctly dodgy, Fletch. On the telephone. He said, *Not to worry, Not to worry*, I was about to start principal photography on a film and I should keep my mind on that, he'd take care of everything else. I was so upset I screened *Being There* three times and *Why Shoot The Teacher?* twice."

"Say, you were upset."

"I called Steve back and told him I was taking the next plane to New York. He squacked and gobbled. By the time I got to the apartment in New York and called him, he'd been called away to Atlanta, Georgia. On business."

"While we're speaking of that, Moxie..."

Her eyes widened at the interruption.

"...You do live pretty well," Fletch said. "You have that big place in Malibu, on the beach, with a pool and screening room. You have that real nice apartment in New York—"

"Look who's talking!" she exclaimed. "A two-bit reporter with a gorgeous place on the Italian Riviera—"

"Oh. That again."

"—who's spent years on a book about some artist—"

"Edgar Arthur Tharp."

She grinned wickedly. "How's the book coming, Fletch?"

"Slowly."

"Slowly! Have you started Chapter Two yet?"

"There have been a lot of distractions."

"I need the house in California, Fletch, for my work. I live there. I need the apartment in New York. For my work. I live there. Neither place is a sun-and-sport *palacia* in Italy!"

"Well, I've had my troubles with the Internal Revenue Service, too."

"No more of your sympathy, thank you. I do believe the Internal Revenue Service, in this case, is right. In New York, I go over to Steve's office, even though I've been told he's not there. Everybody recognizes me, of course. They've been dealing with my stuff for years. I request a quiet office and all the books, all the figures which relate to me and my affairs."

"They had to give them to you."

"They did."

"But why did you ask?"

"Why not? I had to."

"Moxie, there is no way you can understand

such books and figures, as you call them, without training. You needed a professional accountant."

"I could understand enough."

"You could understand nothing."

"For years Steve has been telling me I must borrow money, I must borrow money, being in debt was good for me, paying interest greatly improved my tax situation. I hated the whole thought of being in debt. He explained to me it was just paper debt. So every time he shoved papers in front of me, I signed them. Fletch, I discovered that he had borrowed millions of dollars in my name."

"Entirely possible. Probably right...I think. I don't know either."

"Fletch, what's a tax shelter?"

"It's a little stick house where you go to live once the Internal Revenue Service is done with you."

"He had borrowed money in my name from foreign banks. Geneva, Paris, Mexico City."

"That seems odd. I really don't know."

"He bought stock with my money, all of which seemed to diminish rapidly in value."

"Bad luck."

"Real estate in Atlantic City. A horse farm somewhere, film companies..."

"Moxie, the figures mean nothing to you. They wouldn't mean anything to me either. The way these business types do up their figures is meant to baffle all normal human beings."

"Fletch," she said like a scared child. "I am

millions of dollars in debt. To the banks. To the Internal Revenue Service."

She turned her chair and looked out the window.

Fletch gave her the moment of silence.

Frederick Mooney had opened another bottle from his flight bag and had poured into a champagne glass.

"Oh, look," Moxie said finally. "The moon is rising."

"It is?" Fletch said.

"Perfect timing."

He leaned forward to look through the window. The moon really was rising. "How very romantic of me."

"Right in the right spot in my window, too," she said. "Mister Fletcher, are you trying to seduce me?"

"No. You're too drawn and haggard."

She shrugged. "It's always the ones I'm attracted to who won't have me."

After a while, Fletch asked, "What did Steve Peterman say when you confronted him with all this?"

"Just what you said. That I didn't know what I was talking about, everything was too complicated for me to understand, that after principal photography of the film was over he'd go over the books with me and explain everything."

"And the Internal Revenue Service?"

"He said he'd take care of that."

"And you left everything that way?"

"I spent a week trying to find you. I asked you to come down."

"I'm not an accountant. I wish I were. I see three figures together and suffer vertigo."

"I needed a shoulder to cry on."

"I've got two of them."

"Also, Fletch, I hate to speak well of you to your face but you did have one or two successes as an investigative reporter."

"Only recognized as such in retrospect, I fear."

"You've told me a few things you've done."

"Anything to while away the time."

"I thought maybe I'd get your opinion of Steve Peterman."

"He was an annoying son of a bitch."

Frederick Mooney swiveled around in his chair, to face them. "How could I have been seeing Broadway?" he asked.

"That's a good question," Fletch answered.

"We've been flying over Broadway," Frederick Mooney told his daughter. "The Great White Way. The Star Spangled Street. The Magnificent Road Of Light In An Ocean Of Darkness."

"Oh," Fletch said. "We've been flying over the Florida Keys."

"Well, young man." Frederick Mooney burped. "I suspect we're about to land on Herald Square."

9

"Fletch! What have you done?"

"What do you mean, what have I done?"

In the dark, Moxie was squinting at the airport where they had landed. "Where are we?"

"Here."

"We're not in Fort Myers."

"We aren't?" He was trying to hustle Moxie and Frederick Mooney from the airplane to the taxi stand. Unfortunately there were signs in all the appropriate places saying KEY WEST.

"We're in Key West!" Moxie said.

"We are?" Fletch took Mooney's clanging flight bag from him. "Darned pilot. Must have landed us in the wrong place."

"Union Square?" enquired Mooney.

"What are we doing in Key West?"

Fletch was walking them around the terminal rather than through it. "You said you were tired of Route 41."

"So?"

"All roads end in Key West. Usually in a pile-up."

There were two taxis at the stand.

"Fletch," Moxie said seriously. "That woman. The Chief of Detectives. She told us not to leave the Fort Myers area. At least she told me not to leave the Fort Myers area."

"She mentioned something of the same to me, too."

Moxie faced Fletch on the sidewalk. "Then what are we doing in Key West?"

"Escaping."

"We were told—"

"That has no force in law, you know."

"It hasn't?"

"No. It hasn't. We're not out on bail, or on parole. We haven't been charged with anything."

Frederick Mooney was climbing into the backseat of a taxi.

"Are we fugitives from justice?" she asked.

"Ah, that we may be. It's just that if you run away under such circumstances people are more apt to think you're guilty."

"And we've run away. Great."

"Well, hell, Moxie, aren't you guilty?" Her eyes went from him to the patient taxi driver to Mooney's dark bulk in the backseat. "Not too many people had the opportunity, given the unique circumstances which then prevailed, of sticking ol' Steve. Up there—" Fletch pointed to the sky, "—you gave heavy enough reasons for killing him to bring the airplane down anywhere. Opportunity," Fletch said. "Motive," Fletch said.

"You mean I shouldn't have told you all that?"

"Justification," Fletch said. "Sounded a milimeter away from a confession, to me."

For a moment under the arc lights, Moxie Mooney almost looked drawn and haggard.

"Come on," Fletch said. "Let's go with Freddy. Otherwise, he might not know where he's going."

Moxie sat between them in the backseat of the taxi.

"The Blue House," Fletch said to the driver. "On Duval Street."

The taxi started off.

To Moxie, Fletch said, "I've borrowed a house. From a friend."

Mooney took a drink.

"Listen," Fletch said to Moxie. "A few days of peace and quiet..."

Moxie got out of the taxi while Fletch was paying the driver through the side window. She looked up at the lit house.

"Irwin," she said. "This Blue House is not blue."

"It isn't?"

"Am I going crazy? Even in this light I can tell this Blue House is not blue."

Fletch helped Frederick Mooney out of the taxi.

"Key West is an eccentric town," Fletch said.

"Doubt you'll be here long enough to get used to it."

Moxie hesitated on the sidewalk. She raised her head and spoke to the sky. "What am I supposed to do?"

"Be nice," Fletch answered, helping Mooney up the three steps.

"Mister Peterson," Mooney said at the top of the stairs. "You are a nice young man, but if you don't stop helping me, I will brain you."

"Sorry." Fletch let go of him.

Mooney swayed on the verandah. "You're upsetting my balance."

Moxie followed them through the doorway. "Why is this Blue House white?"

"Jeez," Fletch said. "You couldn't call it The White House. Wouldn't be respectful."

The Lopezes, who took care of The Blue House, were not in the house. Fletch knew they lived in their own house behind the garden wall. The front door had been left unlocked, the lights on. In the dining room a tray of cut sandwiches had been set out along with a fancy ice bucket full of cans of beer. Lights were on even at the back of the house, in the billiard room.

Fletch zipped around the house turning out the lights. "I'll show you to your rooms."

Moxie said, "It's not even nine o'clock."

"Time means nothing in Key West." He started up the stairs. "Never believe a clock in Key West."

Mooney attacked the stairs. "Charge!" he said.

Plodding after him, Moxie said, "Dear O. L.

Your allusion to *Arsenic and Old Lace* under these circumstances is decidedly in poor taste."

Fletch pointed to the first door on the right. "This is your room, Ms Mooney. I think you'll find everything in order. Towels in the bathroom."

She looked into the room and then across the wide corridor at him. "Do I give you a tip?"

"If you have trouble with the air conditioner, just call downstairs."

Fletch pushed open another door. "This room is your's, Mister Mooney. See? Nice big double bed."

"Very good." Frederick Mooney staggered through the door to his room. "What time do I go on?"

"Not to worry," Fletch said. "We'll call you in plenty of time."

"Just did Lear," Fletch heard Mooney muttering through the door. "Must be *Richard III* tonight."

Moxie was standing in the doorway. Even in her black dress, even standing still, her chin tilted slightly up, the light behind her made her presence, her being, exciting.

"Good night, Ms Mooney. Sleep well."

"Good night," she said. "Thanks for bringing my luggage."

Fletch said, "I didn't, did I."

In his own room, Fletch walked out of his moccasins, dropped his shirt and his shorts and his undershorts in a heap on the floor, walked through a warm shower in no time at all, and then walked into bed, fell down, and pulled the sheet over him.

Then he laughed.

10

"I can hardly wait to get old." On the bed, Moxie ran her legs down his and stretched. "Wrinkled and baggy."

"That's what we all want for you," Fletch said.

"I don't mean old," Moxie said. "Just old enough to have an excuse to get fat and ugly."

"Can hardly wait for the day."

She rolled onto her side and faced him, as he was on his side, and their naked bodies were together all the way up and down except for their stomachs. "I can hardly wait to get some roles with some real character in them."

"Belly rolls, uh?"

"Married women, mothers, nuns, grandmothers, business executives. You know what I mean—

women who've lived a little, have some dimension to them and it shows in their faces."

The long door-windows were open to the second-floor balcony and the breeze coming in was slightly humid over their slightly sweaty bodies.

Being Moxie, she had come into his room naked and walked around the room slowly, turning on every light. Her body was totally tanned, as it had to be for her role in *Midsummer Night's Madness*. She had jumped onto his bed, reached down and torn the sheet off him, and then fell on him, flat, jumping to as great a height as she could manage to do so.

Which is why Fletch had turned on his side and they had come to embrace in that position.

"Not like this damned role in *Midsummer Night's Madness*. You know how the scriptwriter wrote in the character for my role? I quote: Beautiful blond female, American build, in twenties, dash Moxie Mooney question mark unquote."

"You sound a natural for the role."

"You call that writing character?"

"Well, you're beautiful, and you're blond, all the way up and down, and you're female, all the way up and down. What's an American build?"

"Guess you're lookin' at it, baby."

"I'm not seeing anything but your eyes, forehead, nose, and cheekbones."

"You're feelin' it, aren't you?"

"Oh, yes. I'm feeling it."

"Feel it some more," she said. "Arr."

"Wait a minute."

"No. Let's not."

*   *   *

Then he was on his back and the breeze seemed cooler to him.

"There are good roles for young people," he said. "There must be."

"Not in *Midsummer Night's Madness*. In *Midsummer Night's Madness* I am body, pure and simple, wide-eyed, innocent, staring, and stupid. All I do is say O! and look alarmed. There are more O's in that script than in ten kilos of Swiss cheese."

"Must be tough bein' just another beautiful face. Body."

Each was spread-eagled on the huge bed, cooling off. Only the tips of their fingers touched.

"Knock it off, Fletcher. I was brought up, trained to do more than stand there and say O! Freddy and I saw to that. I'm not giving you talk-show interview motif number one."

"Sounds it."

For a long moment, she looked at the ceiling. Then she said, "I guess I am. Oh, dear."

"First time you've ever called me dear."

"I didn't call you dear. I called the ceiling dear."

"Watch those expressions of affection, Moxie. Remember, I'm going to have to write to you in the slammer, and our mail will be censored."

"What I'm saying is all this trouble over this film, and the film stinks. Wooden scenes, turgid dialogue, stereotyped characters. All it really is about is people chasing each other along a moonlit beach at night and whumpin' each other."

"Should be a hit."

"Staring Moxie Mooney."

88

"And Gerry Littleford."

"And Gerry Littleford. Not up to his talents either."

"If this film is so bad, Moxie dear, why are you doing it?"

"Steve said I had to. Fulfill some contract or other."

"Fulfill some contract you signed?"

"I signed. Or he signed."

"Seems to me you handed over a large slice of your life to Steve Peterman."

"Fletch, a person in my shoes has to trust somebody."

"You're not wearing shoes. I noticed."

"One cannot be one hundred percent creative sharp and one hundred percent business sharp at the same time. It is mentally and physically impossible. Some people pick wonderful business managers in the talent garden, and live happily ever after. I picked a bad apple."

"And if the District Attorney don't get you, the I.R.S. will."

"You make everything sound so cheery."

"Everything is cheery. It's all in the point of view."

"Want me to tell you about this dumb movie?"

"Yeah. Tell me a story."

"Girl. Got it so far?"

"Yeah. American build. I can see her now."

"Small town."

"Anywhere, U.S.A."

"Anywhere. Gets raped by son of chief of police."

"Opening scene?"

"Opening scene."

"Beats the aerial view of the Empire State Building."

"Of course she doesn't tell."

"Why not?"

"Girls frequently don't tell when they've been raped, Mister Fletcher."

"Why not?"

"It embarrasses them," Moxie said uncomfortably. "It's the psychology of the whole thing. For some crazy reason they think it lowers them in the esteem of others."

"Does it?"

"You tell me. Does it?"

"I hate the whole thought."

"Have you been raped?" she asked.

"Sure."

"Have you told?"

"No."

"Why not?"

"It comes up in conversation so seldom," he said.

"You're not letting me get to the point of the movie."

"Get to the point."

"Girl is pregnant. Girl is truly in love with young black male."

"American build?"

"You've seen Gerry Littleford."

"Handsome man. Looks like a Greyhound. Racing dog, I mean. Not the bus."

"White girl and black man get engaged to be married."

"Does he know she's pregnant by another man?"

"Sure. These people really love each other."

"And what happens?"

"Town finds out they intend to get married. Town not pleased. Give black man a hard time. Town discovers girl is pregnant already. And then on midsummer's night town goes crazy and pursues black man through countryside, swamp, woods until he comes to the edge of the ocean where they catch him and beat him to death. Needless to say, rapist-son-of-police-chief deals the killing blow, right into the black man's head while the black man's head is against a rock."

"Yuck."

"Midsummer Night's Madness."

"It plays upon people's worst emotions, Moxie. It really does."

"Oh, come on, Fletch. People don't think that way anymore. Gerry Littleford's wife is white."

"Yeah. In recent years, miscegenation has been made legal. Most places."

"You mean it's still illegal some places?"

"Yes."

"Come on, Fletch. I've read there is no such thing as an American black person without some white blood."

"We're talking about rape again. Aren't we." Fletch sat up on the bed and put his back against the tall, carved wooden backboard.

"I wasn't even thinking of those things." Moxie rolled over and put her chin in her elbow. "I just think as a movie it stinks. It's badly written. I think the whole thing was written between drinks in The Polo Lounge. By people who don't know anything about boys and girls, men and women, human beings, The South, The North, or America.

The World. Scene for scene, it just doesn't reflect how people regard each other."

"Moxie?"

"I'm still here. In case you hadn't noticed."

"I'm just thinking. The hit-and-run. Peterman. A question some reporter asked, at the police station. Is it possible some one, or some group is trying to stop this film from being made?"

Her one visible eye looked up and down the wrinkled sheet between them. "No."

"Why not?"

"Commit murder to stop a film?"

"I suppose it's possible."

"People are more sophisticated than that." She curved her back and leaned on her elbows. "It's a bad film, Fletch. It will never be released. No one will ever see it."

"Yeah, but no one knows that, yet."

"I'll tell them, if they ask me."

"You will like hell. In fact, let me ask you this: if filming resumes on this turkey film, will you go back on location and continue starring in it?"

"I have to, Fletch. I have no choice."

"Thanks to dear old Steve Peterman."

"Thanks to dear old Steve Peterman," she repeated quietly.

Somewhere in the house a door slammed. A heavy door.

"What was that?" she asked.

"Oh, no," Fletch said.

He jumped off the bed. "Oh, no."

He ran down the stairs and opened the front

door of the house and stepped out onto the porch. He looked down toward the center of Key West.

There was no one in the street except two men walking directly in front of the house.

"Come on all the way out, beautiful!" called one man.

"You're gorgeous!" screamed the other one.

The first one belted the second one, hard. Fletch heard a bottle drop.

He realized he was naked. "Sorry," he said.

He went back in the house and closed the door. Looked in the kitchen. Upstairs, he looked in Frederick Mooney's room.

Returning to his own bedroom, he said, "I guess your father went out for a walk."

"He went out for a drink and some conviviality," Moxie said. "'Conviviality', he calls it."

"Damn."

"What time is it?"

"Stop asking that question in Key West."

"Is it possible to get a drink in Key West at this hour?"

"Are you kidding?"

"I guess it's early yet anyway. I thought you were putting Freddy to bed a little early."

"Damn, damn," Fletch said. "Damn, damn, damn."

"Nice line," Moxie said. "Up there with O, O, O, O. What's the matter with Freddy going out for a drink? Can't keep him in anyway."

"In case it hadn't dawned on you, O, Luminous Two, I was trying to keep your presence in Key West a deep, dark secret."

"Oh," she said.

"The minute Freddy's famous face hits the light of any bar, up goes the telephone receiver to the press."

"Of course," she said.

"Freddy here: Moxie here. Simple equation."

From the bed, she said, "Nice try, sport. Best laid plans, and all that."

"Damn."

"Damn," she said, looking at him as he stood in the middle of the room. "I think you have an American build."

"Yeah," he said. "I was made in the U.S.A."

11

"So how come," Moxie asked very early in the morning in the bright kitchen, "you get to borrow such a nice big house in Key West at a moment's notice?"

Frederick Mooney was asleep in his room. Fletch had checked.

"It belongs to someone I do business with." Carefully, Fletch was trying to make individual omelettes. "A little business. Well, what it comes down to is that I give him money which he feeds to race horses."

"Sounds like a great business."

"The horses like it, I guess."

"Get any manure in return?"

"Nothing but."

"Even in daylight The Blue House is white. First thing I did this morning was run out and check." Moxie was not wearing the only dress she had brought with her. The large backyard of The Blue House was completely walled. "Are you ever going to tell me why it's called The Blue House?"

"Probably."

"But not now, right?"

"Got to be a little mystery in our relationship."

She was squeezing orange juice. "Seems we have quite a big enough mystery to deal with already."

The omelette was sticking to the pan. Fletch turned down the heat.

"So who owns The Blue House?"

"Man named Sills. Ted Sills."

"Sounds vaguely familiar."

"Come to think of it, I met him at a party at your apartment."

"You did?"

"Tall guy. Beer belly. Hair plastered down."

"Right. Sounds like everybody who comes to my parties."

"Trouble is, I found myself having a drink with him later, talking about investing in his race horses. Then, later, spent a week with him at his horse farm, and the weekend here in Key West, where I actually signed some papers."

"How come you're rich?" Moxie asked.

The phone rang.

Automatically, Moxie picked it up. "The Blue House," she said. "Mister Blue isn't here." Then she said, "Hi, Gerry! How did you know I was here?" She looked across the kitchen at Fletch.

96

"It's on the news this morning?...They even say The Blue House, Key West? Rats..." She listened and then said to Fletch, "Gerry Littleford says it was on Global Cable News at six o'clock last night that I had disappeared." She said into the phone, "That's impossible, Gerry. I didn't disappear until eight o'clock." She shook her head at Fletch. "These reporters," she said. "Aren't they awful?...Yeah, I know. Freddy was out on the town in Key West and spilled all. He's a very convivial man, Freddy is..." She turned her back to Fletch. "...Sure, Gerry...sure...Sure you're not just being paranoid, Gerry? Coke does that to you, you know...Sure...Okay, that would be great." She turned to Fletch. "What street are we on?"

"Duval."

"Duval," Moxie said into the receiver. "Oh, by the way, Gerry, will you bring a script of *Midsummer Night's Madness*? I didn't bring one, and I'd like Fletch to read it.... What's a Fletch?" With dancing eyes she looked up and down Fletch's naked body. "A Fletch is a short order cook. He burns eggs in short order. See you."

She hung up and went back to squeezing orange juice. "That was Gerry Littleford. Wants to come down. Says the police and press are hounding him. I said okay. Lots of orange juice."

In the pan, the omelette had gone limp. Fletch turned the heat up again.

They had breakfast at the table on the cistern in the backyard.

"After Key West wakes up a little, " Fletch said,

"I'll go down and buy you some clothes. Make a list of what you need."

She nodded. "These eggs are interesting," she said. "Cooked in layers. Overcooked, undercooked, overcooked, undercooked, all at once. Never had eggs like these before."

"Hope the Lopezes will rescue us, sooner or later."

While Moxie was in the shower, the phone rang again. Fletch answered it.

"'Allo?"

"Ms Moxie Mooney, please. This is Sergeant Frankel, Bonita Police."

"Ms Oxie Hooney? No one here that name. Good bye."

"Where did Ernest Hemingway live?"

"On the street parallel to this. Whitehead Street," Fletch answered. "Great writer. No sense of humor."

Moxie chalked her cue-tip. "What handicap will you give me?"

Fletch triangled the billiard balls. "Have you been playing very much?"

"None at all."

"You play very well. Ten point in a hundred?"

"You flatter me."

"Fifteen?"

"That would be fine but you will beat me."

"Should we play for a stake? You always wished to play for a stake."

"I think we'd better."

"All right. I will give you eighteen points and we will play for a dollar a point."

Moxie commenced to clear the billiard table. "What have you been reading?"

"Nothing," Fletch said. "I'm afraid I am very dull."

"No. But you should read."

"What is there?"

"There is *The Green Hills of Africa*. There is *A Farewell to Arms*."

"No, he didn't."

"What?"

"He didn't say a farewell to arms."

"Then you have been reading?"

"Yes, but nothing recent."

"I thought *The Old Man and The Sea* a very good story of acquivitiveness."

"I don't know about acquivitiveness."

"Poor boy. We none of us know about the soul. Are you *Croyant?*"

"At night."

It became her turn again and she pocketed three balls. "I had expected to become more devout as I grow older but somehow I haven't," she said. "It's a great pity."

"Would you like to live after death?"

"It would depend on the life. This life is very pleasant. I would like to live forever."

"I hope you will live forever."

"Thank you."

Moxie pocketed the last ball. She had won. "You were very kind to play, *Tenente*."

"It was a great pleasure."

"We will walk out together."

                        *   *   *

She was putting the telephone receiver back on
the cradle when he came back into the bedroom.

"That was Geoff McKensie," she said. "He's
driving down. He called from Key Largo. Guess
he was feeling woebegone."

She was wearing the black dress. She looked
hot. He had put on his shorts.

They had heard the Lopezes come into the
house.

"I'll go get you some clothes," he said.

In the foyer of The Blue House, the Lopezes
greeted Fletch.

"Mister Fletcher," said Mrs Lopez. "Good to
have you here again."

Mister Lopez smiled and shook hands and said
nothing.

"Thank you for having everything so nicely
arranged when we arrived last night."

Mrs Lopez took his head in her hands and
kissed him. "But you ate nothing. You left the
sandwiches and drank none of the beer."

"We had something on the plane."

"And this morning I did not make breakfast.
Someone else did."

"We tried to clean up our mess."

"I can tell."

"Upstairs is a young woman and her father.
And I guess one or two more will be coming for
lunch. We can use the sandwiches you made."

"I'll make something fresh."

"I'm going down to the stores," Fletch said.

"Do you want me to go with you?" Lopez asked.

"No," Fletch said. "Just picking up a few things. Until later."

"Until later," said Mrs Lopez.

12

When he returned, walking slowly down Duval Street in the sunlight and warm wind, his arms ladened with packages, there were two cars with their trunks open in front of The Blue House. It had taken Fletch much longer to shop for Moxie than he had expected. Originally, there was confusion in the salesman's mind. Clearly he wanted to think Fletch was buying this feminine clothing for himself, and clearly he wanted to play with Fletch in the process.

The short, weather-beaten man Fletch had seen in the police station was unloading a small yellow car. Apparently he had travelled alone. A large blue sedan was disgorging Edith Howell, the actress who could and did look like everybody's mother, and John Meade, who could not stop looking like a hayseed even when he wasn't being paid to do so. They had much luggage. Fletch had not been told to expect Edith Howell and John Meade.

Across the street a small group of tourists, cameras around some necks, stood in a loose group, to watch and chat with each other over what they were and were not seeing. A tourist road-train was crawling by in the street. The tour guide was saying through his amplifier:...*Blue House. In residence now in The Blue House is the actress, Moxie Mooney, and her father, the legendary Frederick Mooney. Now the Blue House is being used as a hide out for these celebrities who just yesterday were present when someone literally, really, troo-ooly got murdered on The Dan Buckley Show. Arrived late last night in time for old Frederick to grab a few quick ones in the local bistros. Maybe I shouldn't point out their hideout to you, but the fact that they're there is in all the morning newspapers. Coming up on your left...*

The front door of The Blue House was wide open.

Moxie was in the dining room stacking a tall pile of napkins. "Thank God," she said, seeing the packages in Fletch's arms. "I'm broiled and baked."

"You have more guests arriving," Fletch said. "Edith Howell. John Meade."

"Yeah. They called from Key Marathon."

"Geoff McKensie. I think."

"You knew he was coming." She was tearing through the packages on the diningroom table.

"More in the backyard. Gerry Littleford and his wife. Sy Koller flew down with them."

"Sy Koller? We have two directors in the house? Isn't that like having two ladies wearing the same expensive dress?"

Moxie was holding the bottom of a yellow bikini against her black dress. "I think it will fit."

"I just ordered for the American build. Where is everyone going to sleep?"

"There are couches, hammocks, swings on all the balconies."

"Where's Oh, Luminous One?"

"Gone out for some conviviality."

"This house lacks conviviality? It's about to burst with conviviality. Moxie, my idea of getting you away for a few days—"

"I am away. I don't need to hide out." Vexed, she was pincering all the packages from the table against her breasts. "I didn't murder anybody, you know."

"Then we'd better find another suspect," said Fletch. "Damned quick. And it's not going to be easy to find a better suspect than you are."

"I'll go change." She dashed out of the dining room and headed for the stairs. "You go meet the people."

Fletch carried a glass of orange juice into the backyard.

Gerry Littleford was the first to see him. "You're a Fletch," he said.

"Right."

"I'm Gerry." He stood up to shake hands. "This is my wife, Stella."

Stella was the young woman who the day before had taken Marge Peterman in hand.

"You know Sy Koller?"

The heavy man in the stressed T-shirt had also been kind to Marge Peterman the day before. Today's stressed T-shirt was green. He did not rise for Fletch or offer his hand. "I'm sorry," he said to Fletch.

"You're a cook?" Gerry sat down again.

"Moxie only said that before she tried my omelette."

"Not afterwards?"

"No. Not afterwards."

Everyone in the group had a Bloody Mary.

"I really am sorry," Koller said again. His eyes said he was sorry.

"Sorry for what?" Fletch sat in one of the white, wrought-iron, cushioned love seats. It was cooler in the walled garden, without the warm Gulf wind.

"For turning you down for that part."

"You never did."

Koller looked relieved and grinned. "I was sure I had. By my age, son, a director has turned down almost everybody. What have you done?"

"Done?"

"What films have you been in?"

"I'm not an actor."

"But I've seen your work."

"You saw me yesterday. On Bonita Beach. I was with Marge Peterman."

Koller continued to stare at him.

105

"Illusion and reality," Gerry Littleford said. "It's an occupational hazard. Confusion between what we see and do on the screen and what we see and do in real life. What is real and what is on film?"

"It's a sickness of the whole society," Stella said. "There is no reality for people now unless they do see it on film."

Gerry said, "It's our job to make what happens on film appear more real than reality."

"And sometimes," Sy Koller said, "we succeed."

"Was yesterday real?" Stella asked. "Or just a segment on *The Dan Buckley Show?*"

"I don't know," Sy Koller laughed. "I haven't seen it on television yet. I'll tell you after I do."

Gerry Littleford ran his eyes over the banyan tree. "Is today real?" His arm rested on the back of the love seat, behind his wife's head.

"Any day I'm not working, creating unreality," Sy Koller said quietly, "is not real."

"Yesterday..." Gerry said.

Through the back door of the house came Edith Howell, Geoff McKensie, and John Meade. Each was carrying a Bloody Mary. The Lopezes were being kept busy.

Koller jumped up. "Geoff!" He tripped on the edge of the cistern greeting McKensie. "This is great! I've been hoping we'd get some time together."

"You mean before I shove off?"

"You were pushed off," said Koller. "Something similar's happened to me. More than once. Come on into the shade."

Everyone greeted everyone else with kisses, except McKensie, who kissed no one. Gerry Littleford introduced Fletch.

Edith Howell acknowledged the introduction by saying, "I didn't know what to do with my bags, dear."

Fletch looked doubtfully at her breasts and she sat down on a wicker chair.

John Meade said, "Good afternoon. Are you our host?"

"I guess so."

"Thank you for having us."

Geoffrey McKensie said nothing. He did not shake hands. But looking at Fletch his eyes clicked like the shutter of a camera's lens.

"The light you got in *The Crow*—fantastic!" Koller walked McKensie to two chairs at the back of the group. "Particularly in that last scene, the final scene with the old woman and the boy. How did you do it?" He laughed. "Do I have to go to Australia to get light like that?"

"What a dreadful drive," Edith Howell said. "On that seven mile bridge I thought my heart would plop into the water."

"Is that why you never stopped talkin'?" Meade asked with a grin.

"As long as one is talking," Edith Howell said, "one must be alive. Is Freddy here?" she asked Fletch.

"He's here somewhere. Guess he went for a walk."

"My, how that man wanders," said Edith.

In the fan-backed wicker chair instinctively Edith Howell seemed to take over the foreground. Gangly in a light iron chair, John Meade seemed to fill up the background. In his eager manners, in his absorbing everything around him, Gerry Littleford always looked ready to go on. The other non-professional among them, Stella Littleford, had a cute face but was small and white to the point of sallowness. The way she slumped in her chair put her very much offstage.

"What a magnificent house," Edith Howell said. "Looks so cool and airy. You must tell us all about Key West," she said to Fletch. "How long have you lived here?"

"About eighteen hours."

"Oh." She wrinkled her nose at the back of the house. "It's called The Blue House...Maybe the front of it's blue. I didn't notice."

"It isn't," said Fletch.

John Meade laughed. "You sure are a good ol' boy, aren't you?"

Moxie popped out the back door wearing the new yellow bikini. There were more hugs and kisses. She kissed both Sy Koller and Geoffrey McKensie.

She sipped Fletch's orange juice. "There's no vodka in it."

"There isn't?"

"How can you make a Screw Driver without vodka?" she asked.

"You can't," he said.

John Meade laughed.

Moxie sat in the love seat beside Fletch. "Don't tell me. You're all talking shop."

"Stella and I were talking about fishing," Fletch said.

"Now that you bring it up," John Meade drawled. "Sy? Are we going to finish the film?"

Sy looked at Moxie. "I wish I knew."

And Moxie said: "That depends on the banks, doesn't it? If the bankers say we finish, we finish. If the bankers say we don't finish, we don't finish. Jumping Cow Productions."

"Yeah," said Koller. "That's the reality of this business. The only reality."

Littleford said, "We needed a break from filming anyway." He rubbed his left forearm. "I was gettin' weary of gettin' beat up. Give my bruises a chance to heal."

The Lopezes appeared and began handing around trays of sandwiches.

Edith Howell put her hand on Moxie's knee and said, quietly, "I hope it was all right for us to come, dear. I suppose we were all thinking the same thing..." Moxie's eyes widened. "...At a time like this, you need people around you. Friends."

Moxie stared at her, open-mouthed.

"Have a sandwich," Fletch said. Lopez had placed the fancy beer-ice cooler in the shade. "Have a beer. Want me to get you a beer?"

Moxie didn't answer.

Everyone but Moxie had a sandwich and drink in hand. The Lopezes had returned to the house.

Moxie stood up. She said, slowly, distinctly, "Dear friends. I did not kill Steve Peterman. Anyone who isn't sure of that fact is free to leave."

In the heavy silence, Moxie walked back to the house. She let the back door slam behind her.

Stella Littleford muttered, "That would leave an empty house."

"Shut up," her husband said. He looked apologies at Fletch, and at Sy Koller.

Fletch cleared his throat. "Someone bumped the son of a bitch off."

Stella said, "He probably deserved it. The bastard."

"I have my own theory." Sy Koller waited for everyone's attention. "Dan Buckley."

"That's a good theory," said Fletch.

"He was as close to him as Moxie was."

"You're just saying that," Gerry said to Sy, "because he was the only one present not..." He waved his sandwich at the group under the banyan tree. "...not one of us. Not working with us."

"No." Sy Koller was munching his sandwich. "I know they knew each other. Before. How else do you think Steve Peterman got Buckley to tape his show on location? Buckley doesn't cart himself around to every film location, you know."

Fletch asked, "What else do you know?"

"Well, I know Peterman was to have dinner with Buckley. To discuss business. I'm pretty sure they had done business together. Buckley kept referring to some aluminum mine in Canada, throwing significant looks at Peterman, and Peterman kept smiling and changing the topic of conversation."

"That would be nice." Fletch looked at each of them. "If it were Dan Buckley."

"Sure," Sy Koller said. "Tell me this: who else could have rigged his own set? I speak as a director." He looked at Geoffrey McKensie for confirmation. "A director is responsible for everything that happens on a set. He's the only one who really understands everything on a set, what everything is for, how everything works. As a director I say—take a simple, open set like the one for *The Dan Buckley Show* and get a knife to fall accurately enough and with enough force to get into somebody's back and kill him—that's not easy. You can't rig that in two minutes flat. It had to be Dan Buckley."

"Or someone on his crew," said Meade.

"Did the knife fall?" asked Fletch.

Koller said, "I don't know. Obviously it came from somewhere with force. I was thinking about this all night. I'm sure I could rig that set to put a knife in somebody's back." Generously, he turned to McKensie. "I'm sure Geoff here could, too. But I couldn't figure the best way to do it after thinking about it all night." Summarily, he said: "I think Buckley's the only one who could have had that set primed and working for him yesterday. To kill Peterman."

In the digestive silence, the amplified voice of a tour guide wafted over the back wall. "... *Mooneys, famous father and famous daughter, being questioned by police regarding the murder yesterday of somebody on the set of* The Dan Buckley Show. *The old man doesn't seem too upset. Hour ago I saw him downtown crossin' the street from Sloppy Joe's to Captain Tony's ...*

"Aw, turn it off," McKensie said. "Makes me sick."

Edith Howell again was pointing her nose at the back of The Blue House. "At least," she said, "it's nice to get away from hotel living for a few days."

13

Fletch pushed open the door with his foot and carried the tray into his mid-day darkened bedroom. On the tray were a few cut sandwiches, a pitcher of orange juice and a glass. He placed the tray on the bedside table.

Moxie was an X on the bed. She had removed her bikini top.

"I didn't kill Steve," she said.

"We have to find who did, Moxie. You're seriously implicated. Or, you're going to be. Once the facts come out. I mean, about your funny financial dealings with Peterman."

" 'Financial dealings'. I didn't even understand them. I trusted the bastard, Fletch." She groaned. "Millions of dollars in debt."

"I know you didn't understand them. I understand you had to trust someone. Either you had to
be a creative person, or a business person. You
had an opportunity to throw yourself one hundred percent into your creative life, and it was
good for everybody that you did."

"Don't judges and people like the I.R.S. understand that sort of thing? It's not hard to understand."

"Not in this country, anyway. In this country,
everything is a business. Being creative is a business. Except you don't have any executive staff,
board of directors, business training or experience
to fall back on. That's all your fault, you see,
because being creative here is really being nothing. In America, a creative person is only as good
as his income. When you sign something, it signifies
you understand what you're signing. And you're
solely responsible for what you've signed."

"But Goddamn it, it happens all the time. You
read about it—"

"So you have to protect yourself."

"So Steve Peterman was supposed to protect
me."

"So maybe he screwed you."

"And that's what happens all the time. Jeez,
Fletch."

"Ignorance is no defense in the law, they say.
More to the point, it's almost impossible to prove
you didn't know what you didn't know. Playing
dumb is a courtroom cliche."

"Courtroom! O-oh. You had to use that word,
didn't you?"

"Sorry." He sat on the bed. "Trouble is, you see,

you did understand something. You arrived in Steve Peterman's office, during his absence, and went through his books. Two weeks later, sitting next to you, he gets stabbed to death."

There was a long silence in the darkened room. Her eyes roamed the ceiling. She sighed. "Looks bad."

"Moxie, I have a friend in New York, a good friend, who is both a lawyer and a Certified Public Accountant. I believe in this person. He'll need your written permission, but I'd like him to review your books in Steve Peterman's office. So we'll know how much financial trouble you're really in."

"What does it matter? They're going to try me for murder."

"There's a chance—a small chance—you read the books all wrong. That Steve represented you well. That you have no complaints. That you had no motive to murder him."

"Fat chance."

"It's worth a shot. And if the news is bad, it's proven you did have a motive to murder him—"

"Don't tell me. Just lead me to the execution chamber."

"—then at least we'll know that. We have to move fast on this. I expect the authorities will want a look at those books, too. We want to beat them to it."

"What do you want me to do?"

"Sign this piece of paper." He took a paper from the pocket of his shorts and unfolded it. "Giving my friend, Marty Satterlee, permission to review your financial accounts." He took a pen from another pocket.

"Okay." She sat up and signed the paper on his knee.

"I'll call him immediately and send a messenger up to New York with your written permission."

"Send a messenger to New York?"

"There must be someone in Key West who wouldn't mind a free ride to the big city and back."

"Wow. Sounds like you're in the movie business."

"No," Fletch said. "This is serious business."

She lay back on the bed. The back of her hand was on her brow. "Bunch of savages downstairs," she said.

"You seemed glad enough to see them."

"I never thought—until Edith gave me those pastoral eyes—they'd all think I murdered Steve. If they think I murdered someone, why are they so eager to come stay in the same house with me?"

"I don't know," Fletch said. "Maybe because they're friends." Moxie snorted. "Well, their being here is a gesture of support."

"When I want support," Moxie said, "I'll buy a girdle."

"No need for that yet, old thing." His hand passed over her breasts and stomach and hips. "But you might work on it." He picked up the plate of sandwiches. "Cream cheese and olive?"

"No. I just want a nap."

He put down the plate. "Orange juice?"

"No."

"Want company?"

"Just want to sleep. Stop thinkin'. Stop painin'."

"Okay. Hey, Moxie, that Roz Nachman—remember who she is?"

"Yeah. The Chief of Detectives."

"She's one smart, tough woman, I think. I expect we can have some faith in her."

"Okay," Moxie said. "If you say so."

Before Fletch opened the door, Moxie said, "Fletch?"

"Yeah?"

"What do I do about the funeral? I should go to Steve's funeral."

"I don't know."

"I can't stand the thought of it."

"Send flowers. Poison ivy. That will look good in court."

"I'm thinking of Marge."

"Moxie, darlin', in case you haven't got the point of all my fancy-dancin' the last twenty-four hours, right now you have to think about yourself."

There was a moment's silence from the bed. Then she said. "Just now I'd like to stop thinkin'."

"Oh, and Moxie, hate to hit you when you're down, but, one more thing..." There was complete silence from the bed. "...You just signed a piece of paper in a dark room. You didn't even try to read it." The silence from the bed continued. "You ought to stop doing things like that, Marilyn. Sleep well."

14

"Marty? Fletch. I'm in Key West with Moxie Mooney."

Marty Satterlee said nothing. The conversational was not Marty's style. He received information. He waited until the information he had seemed complete. Then he processed the information. Then he acted upon it. Then he dispensed information.

"In a few hours," Fletch continued, "the actor, John Meade, will be in your office with a piece of paper signed by Moxie giving you authority to examine her financial records in Steve Peterman's office." Fletch explained the rest: that Steve Peterman had been stabbed to death while sitting next to Moxie, and that Moxie worried that her financial affairs, which Peterman had been managing, might be in such disarray as to provide her, in the eyes of the law, with a motive for murdering him. "Will you do it, Marty? As you can see, it's a matter of death or a life's sentence, to coin a phrase." Fletch paused, wondering if he had provided enough information for Marty to go seek more. "Oh, yeah," Fletch added. "There's an element of haste here. John Meade very kindly has offered to fly up to New York with the paper giving you authority to act. He's leaving presently. I expect the police will want a look at these same records. They're probably in court getting permission now."

There was another pause. Fletch believed the information he had given was up to the instant. "How long does it take to discover someone's been playing fast and loose with financial records, Marty?"

"Sometimes hours. Sometimes months."

"Never minutes?"

"Never minutes."

Fletch looked through the door into the billiard room. "Will you do this, Marty? Please?"

Marty Satterlee said, "I'll get some people to help me."

"Thank you, Marty. Please call the instant you have anything."

Fletch gave Marty the telephone number of The Blue House.

Fletch was just standing up from the desk in the small library of The Blue House when the telephone rang.

"Buena," he said into the phone. *"Casa Azul."*

"Fletch!"

"No 'sta 'qui."

"I know it's you, you bastard. You hang up and I'll twist your head off."

"Ted?" Fletch said. "Ted Sills? Nice of you to call home."

"I want—"

"I know. Like the good landlord you are, you want to know if we found everything in the house to our satisfaction—towels in the bathrooms, clean sheets on the beds, coffee in the cupboards—"

"Screw that."

"The Lopezes are marvelous people. We couldn't have felt more welcome."

"I want you—"

"I bet you want to tell me another of my expensive four-legged sacks of glue won another important horse race."

"Fletcher!"

"How much did I win this time? Two dollars and thirty-five cents?"

"Fletcher, I want you out of that house and I mean right now."

"Ted, you sound serious."

"I am serious! I want you out within the hour!"

"Gee, did I do something wrong, Ted? Use too much hot water? Didn't know you had a problem."

"None of your bull, Fletcher. I saw on TBS you're running a circus in The Blue House. In my house! Frizzlewhit said he heard something about it on the morning news. I couldn't believe it. You said you wanted to get away for a few days."

"I am away. Trying to relax from the strain of being a race horse owner."

"Moxie Mooney! Jeez!"

"Sleeping in your bed at the moment. Doesn't that just make your old loins jump though?"

"Frederick Mooney!"

"You'll need a new placard for the front door: *Mooneys, pere et—*"

"Get them out of my house!"

"Why, Ted, their staying here increases the re-sale value of your property by at least, I'd say, another twelve thousand dollars."

"Fletcher." Sills spoke with the deliberation of a poker player playing his ace. "You've drawn a murder investigation to my house."

"Oh, that."

"That."

"That will all come out in the wash."

"What? What did you say?"

"Really, you should be here, Ted, if only you could afford the room rent. Edith Howell is here. John Meade is in and out. Gerry Littleford. Sy Koller. Geoff McKensie."

"You're running a hotel for murder suspects! Fugitives from justice!"

"Ted, why take it so personally? They've got to be somewhere."

"Not in my house, damn it. I want you and that whole gang of murder celebrities out of The Blue House and I mean now. Within the hour."

"No."

"No? What do you mean 'no'?"

"You're forgetting something, Ted."

"I'll never forget this."

"You're forgetting I didn't borrow your house. I'm paying rent for it. If you had been kind, and let me borrow your house, of course I'd have no choice but to accede to your wishes. But as a rent payer, I have certain rights—"

"You're not a rent-payer, you bastard. I never got the check."

"No? The check is in the mail."

"The deal isn't complete. I never got the check. You don't have anything to prove you sent the check."

"But, Ted, I'm in the house. That means something."

"It means you're a guest. And I'm throwing you out."

"Hell of a way to treat a guest."

"I never got the check for the feed bills, either."

"That's coming in dimes and quarters. Look for the truck."

"Fletcher, just hear me out. I let you have The Blue House—"

"At an outrageous rent."

"I didn't want you to have it at all. You never told me you were going to fill the house up with fugitives from a murder investigation."

"Actually, that wasn't my intention."

"It's my house. My home. I don't want pictures of it all over the world on the front pages of police gazettes and scandal magazines."

"Never knew you were so sensitive."

"Get out. Get out. Get those people out of there. Get everybody out of that house. Instantly."

The phone went dead.

Fletch looked into the phone's mouthpiece. "Great instrument of communication," he muttered to himself. "Designed for those who insist upon having the last word."

Mrs Lopez was in the door of the study. "Anything you want, Mister Fletcher?"

"No, thanks, Mrs. Lopez."

"Coffee? Cold drink?"

Fletch picked up the script of *Midsummer Night's Madness* from the desk. "Maybe I'll pick up a cold drink as I go through the kitchen."

She smiled. "Everyone is napping now."

"Everyone except Mister Meade. He's about to run an errand."

"Me, too," she said. "Shopping. It's nice having so many people in the house. So many people I've only seen in the movies." The woman fluttered her hand in a girlish gesture. "That Mister Mooney! What a man. What a gentleman!"

"You know about the murder?"

She shrugged. "Last night there was another murder. Up the block. Behind the house." Her hand indicated southwest. "A man was stabbed. So it goes. The tour trains are not announcing that murder."

"Why was he stabbed?"

Again Mrs Lopez shrugged. "He said something. Or he said nothing. He did something. Or he did nothing. He had something. Or he had nothing. Why are people murdered?"

"Or because he was something."

"*Tambien.* Any special foods you like me to get?"

"Good fruit," Fletch said. "Fish. Some cheese?"

"Of course. For how many days should I buy?"

"For a few days," Fletch said. "For a few days at least."

15

While Fletch was reading page 81 of the *Midsummer Night's Madness* filmscript, a woman screamed.

Sitting in the back garden of The Blue House he looked up at the second storey.

It had been Edith Howell who screamed. Now she was shouting. Despite the theatrical timber of her voice, Fletch could not make out what she was saying.

He turned to page 82.

It was a drowsy afternoon.

When Fletch was on page 89, Frederick Mooney stumbled around the corner of the house. He stood in a patch of ground cover.

"There is what says she is a lady in my bed," Frederick Mooney announced.

"Is that a complaint?" Fletch asked.

"I'd rather a woman," admitted Mooney.

"It's Edith Howell," said Fletch.

"Is that who it was? I thought I recognized her from some similar scene...let's see, was it *The Clock Struck One?*"

"And down fell the other one?"

"Neither a lady nor a woman: Edith Howell." Mooney's feet tangled in the ground cover as he stepped forward. "Umbrage in feminine flesh."

"She asked for you the minute she arrived."

Mooney lowered himself into a shaded wrought-iron chair. "I think we did a play together once. Can't think what. At least, I remember seeing her night after night for an extended period. You know, like a hotel bathtub."

"You did *Time, Gentlemen, Time* together. On Broadway."

"Oh, yes—that damned musical. How did I ever come to do that damned musical? I was miserable in it for months...although the audience seemed to like it. Bad advice, I guess. Are you a theater buff?"

"No more than anyone else."

"Always amazing to me how much other people know about theater and films than I do."

Fletch smiled. "You are theater and films, Mister Mooney."

"I've done my job," Mooney said. "Like anyone else. If I remember correctly, Mister Peterkin, you

125

said you have nothing to do with the entertainment *hindustry*."

"Right. I don't."

Mooney tried to read the title of the filmscript on Fletch's lap. *"Midsummer Night's Dream,"* he said. *"Call you me fair?"* he said in a sad, light voice. *"I am as ugly as a bear.* Marvelous the annual income Sweet Will still produces. He should be around to enjoy it."

"Midsummer Night's Madness," Fletch said. "The film Moxie is now doing."

"Oh, yes. Shakespeare in modern togs, I suppose. With this year's psychiatric understandings thrown in."

"No." Fletch bounced the script on his knee. "There seems no relation between the two midsummer nights."

"Just cribbing the title, eh? Wonder someone hasn't written a play called *Piglet,* 'bout a chap who sees the ghost of last night's supper. Alas, poor supper, I ate you well..."

"Moxie hasn't talked to you about this script?"

"Moxie does not talk to me." Mooney hiccuped behind his hand. "Moxie does not seek my advice. I am her drunken father. 'Tis well and just, I say. There were many years when I was caused to ignore her."

"What caused that?"

Mooney's eyes approached Fletch from both sides of his head, and consumed him. "Talent is the primary obligation," said he. "Many men can love a woman and produce children; few can love the world and produce miracles."

Fletch nodded. "Mind if I seek your advice?"

Mooney said neither yes nor no. He searched the ground around his chair. He had not brought his bag of bottles. He had been convivial in the bars of Key West since before lunch, though.

"Why would anyone make a bad movie?" Fletch asked.

"It's like any other business," Mooney said. "People make mistakes. No. Allow me to amend that. No other *hindustry* operates with such a stupifyingly high mistake factor. Could you run your business, Mister Peterkin, with a ninety percent error factor?"

"How could that be?"

"Making a good film means bringing together exactly the right talents with exactly the right material. Not an easy job."

"I still don't get it. No business can keep running if ninety percent of everything it does is wrong."

"And then I can point out to you—as a bitter, burned out old man, mind you—that any business of glamour and big bucks attracts to it more than its share of incompetents and charlatans."

Fletch tried to wrap his eyes around Mooney. "Why should you be bitter?"

"Because I have had more than my share of incompetents and charlatans ruining my sleep and my waking, damaging my work, advising me ill, treating me badly, robbing me—"

"Ho down," said Fletch. "Didn't mean to heat your blood. Too hot a day for that."

Mooney inhaled deeply through his nose. He turned his profile to Fletch and exhaled slowly. Fletch wondered if such was an actor's exercise.

"I don't see how any business—or *hindustry*, as you call it—can run with such a high failure ratio."

Mooney's smile was sardonic. "There are many ways this business operates. The simple answer to your question is that just often enough the right materials come together with the right talents. The miracle of art happens. Even people like you put down your barbells and rush out, money in hand, crazed to see what mammon has wrought. And its payday for the *hindustry*. A single flash of light in the night makes safe the dark."

"I'm just reading this filmscript." Fletch jiggled his knee under it. "I don't know, of course. Never read a filmscript before. It strikes me as pretty terrible. The characters all seem to be like people you meet at a cocktail party—all fronts and no backs. They don't talk the way people really talk. I do a little writing myself—on days when there are hurricanes. It seems to me, in this filmscript much time and space are wasted while the author is floundering around trying to arrive at an idea. All that should be cut away. Don't you think writing should begin after the idea is achieved?" Mooney was looking at him like a bull bored with the pasture. "It treats controversial old issues in an insulting, offensive way. Instead of trying to create any sort of understanding, my reading of it is that it is trying to provoke hatred—deliberately." Again Mooney was surveying the ground around his chair for the bottle bag. "Not a critic of filmscripts, of course," Fletch said. "But I think anyone would have to be crazy to invest a dime in this rubbish."

"Ah, Peterkin," said Mooney, obviously sitting on his own restlessness. "You just said the magic word: *dime*. Like any other business, the film *hindustry* is about money. Lots of it. Consider this: never does so much money come together over the creation of an illusion." Mooney moved to get out of his chair but did not make it. "Think about that, if you will. Count your illusions, Mister Peterkin." Finally, Mooney succeeded in standing up. "The time for a nap has passed," he announced to the banyan tree, which never napped. "I need a drink to smooth the wrinkles of my day. May I bring you one, Peterson?"

Slowly, he hoped in a theatrical manner, Fletch squinted all around him before asking, "Who's Peterson?"

"Why, you're Peterson, aren't you? Oh, I'm sorry. Peterkin. You're Peterkin. You just said that, I believe. You should have seen an early film of mine, *Seven Flags*."

"I have."

"Cast of thousands," said Mooney. "And I kept every one of them straight."

16

Lopez called from the back door. "Telephone, Mister Fletcher."

Fletch hesitated. The phone had been ringing all day. Fletch had told the Lopezes to try not to answer it. He dropped the filmscript of *Midsummer Night's Madness* onto the cistern and trudged to the back door.

"Sorry." Lopez's eyes sought sympathy, understanding. "It is the police. The woman insists you come to the phone. She threatened me."

A babble of voices was coming from inside the house.

"Okay."

Stella Littleford passed Fletch on her way out the back door. "Watch out," she whispered.

In the corridor, Edith Howell asked, "Where's Freddy?"

"Don't know. Here somewhere."

"Where's John Meade?"

"Gone on an errand. He'll be back."

In the front hall, dressed only in bikini underpants, Gerry Littleford stood with his back against the wall. "I don't know." He shook his head sadly. "I don't know."

Through the open front door, Fletch saw the waiting, staring crowd across the street had grown.

Frederick Mooney was coming down the stairs. He held a bottle by its neck.

Behind Fletch, Edith Howell exclaimed, "Freddy! Why, I do declare! As I live and breathe!"

Halfway down the stairs, Mooney focused on her. He pointed at her. *This old moon wanes...*"

"Come make me a drink, lover. I'm parched." She took his arm as he came off the stairs. "A gin and tonic would be nice." She walked him into the living room. "I found some supplies in here. Sorry I spoke so harshly to you, when you burst into my bedroom, but, Freddy, it's been so many years since you did such a thing..."

As they passed him, Gerry Littleford said to the floor, "I don't know."

"Madame," Mooney's voice rang regally from the living room. "I do not burst. I enter."

In the billiard room, Moxie was turning in circles. "Fletch! I've got to get out of this house!"

"You can't."

"I can't stand it!"

"You'd be mobbed. It wouldn't be safe."

She emphasized every word. "I have to get out of this house!"

Fletch went into the study and picked up the telephone receiver. "Hello?"

"Irwin Fletcher?"

Fletch sighed. "This is Fletcher."

"One moment, please."

From overhead came Sy Koller's heavy voice. He was saying something about the Gulf Stream.

"Mister Fletcher," a voice stated through the telephone.

"Yes."

"This is Chief Nachman. How are you today?"

"Fine. Thank you. Yourself?"

"Fine. Hard works always makes one feel better, don't you think?"

"Glad to hear you're working hard."

"Are you?"

"You bet."

"My hard work may result in some conclusions you're not going to like."

"No way."

"Which is why you flew Ms Mooney to the ends of the earth last night."

"We're not that far away."

"You're in a place where it is very simple for you to skip the country."

"You noticed that."

"Yes and no. Don't push me too far, Irwin."

"You don't need to call me Irwin."

"You don't like the name Irwin?"

"Kids in school used to call me earwig."

"All right, I'll call you earwig."

"That's not what I meant."

"If, for example, you and Ms Mooney were to leave the state of Florida, or worse, much worse, continental U.S.A.—"

"Wouldn't think of it."

"—you would find out what a little ol' Chief of Detectives can do. Your disappearing to Key West with a good many of my suspects in this murder case is an inconvenience for me—only that. Understandable, considering the people involved."

"You're being reasonable."

"Furthermore, I think you may have done the right thing."

"I have?"

"Yes. Maybe. I have a funny feeling you've done exactly the right thing. Now, if you'll be good enough to tell me exactly who is with you down there in—what's it called—The Blue House?"

"Moxie."

"Did you know The Blue House is the name of the Korean presidential residence?"

"Frederick Mooney."

"I'd love to see it someday."

"Gerry Littleford. His wife, Stella. Sy Koller. Edith Howell. The Australian director, Geoffrey McKensie."

"John Meade?"

"He's in and out. He'll be back tonight."

"Didn't you just love him in *Easy River*?"

"Don't think I ever saw it."

"Anyone else?"

"Me."

"I wouldn't forget you, earwig."

"Seeing you're being so reasonable, Chief, would you mind telling me a few things?"

"If I can. Will I see it on Global Cable News?"

"Not if you don't want."

"Your loyalties have their priorities, right, Fletcher?"

"What has shown up, so far, on the tapes and films of the murder?"

"Nothing."

"Nothing?"

"Absolutely nothing. We've been up looking at them all night, over and over. Absolutely nothing."

"That's impossible."

"The murder might as well have taken place in an alley in the dark of night, for all the good all those cameras have done us so far. We're having experts come in to look at the films. Did you know there were experts to look at film? I didn't."

"And probably experts at choosing those experts."

"That's true."

"Wouldn't Sy Koller and Geoff McKensie be able to help? They must be expert at looking at film."

"Great. Two of our prime suspects you want called in as experts. Peterman fired McKensie, you know."

"And Koller?"

"Three years ago Sy Koller and Steve Peterman had a fist fight outside a Los Angeles restaurant. Koller had Peterman on the sidewalk and was strangling him when the police arrived. Peterman did not press charges."

"Everybody loved Peterman. For sure. What were they fighting about?"

"A woman, they said."

"By the way, Koller says Peterman and Dan Buckley knew each other. That there was some tension between them."

"You see? You have the makings of a good earwig. Buckley was losing money in some investment Peterman had gotten him into."

"A lot of money?"

"How do I know what's a lot of money to these people? I live in a yellow bungalow six miles from the beach."

"Okay. Point two. This morning Sy Koller said the set for *The Dan Buckley Show* could have been rigged. That is, the knife could have been made to fall from somewhere, could have been propelled from somewhere, mechanically. You know what I mean?"

"We've thought of it."

"I mean, isn't that the way stages work? The stage set itself creates the illusion. Anything can be built into it. Anything can be made to happen."

"We've looked."

"The fact that nothing shows up on the tapes and films so far sort of substantiates his theory, doesn't it? I mean, this thing would have to be rigged by someone who knew where the cameras would be."

"It's a good theory."

"And Koller points out really the only person who would have the time, the expert knowledge, enough control over the set to rig such a thing would be Dan Buckley himself."

"You notice something?"

"What?"

"Koller seems very anxious to pin Dan Buckley."

"Maybe so. But maybe he's right."

"Last night and again this morning we went over that set millimeter by millimeter."

"Come on, Chief. What does your average cop know about stage sets? Your average citizen can be fooled by an eight-year-old magician wearing French cuffs."

"Which is why we have three set designers flying down from New York."

"Experts."

"More experts. This case is going to wreck our budget for this year, and next. Of course, having to call Key West long distance doesn't help the budget any, either."

"You have film experts coming in and stage set experts."

"We have."

"You know what this means..."

"It means property taxes will have to go up in this district. Because a bunch of rich film people visited us, and one of them got murdered."

"If you need theater experts to solve this crime, then it means this crime must have been committed by a theater expert."

"Very good, earwig. Especially seeing you're the only person involved who has nothing to do with theater."

People were shouting in the front hall of The Blue House.

"I didn't kill Peterman," Fletch said. "You should have asked."

"We're hiring experts by the planeload, Mister Fletcher," Chief Roz Nachman said. "And I intend to listen to them. I also intend to keep my mind open to the simple explanation."

"Which is?"

"I wish I knew. Someone put a knife in Steven Peterman's back. Granted, it happened under most unusual and complicated circumstances. But it is still a simple crime of violence."

"Anything I can do to help?"

"Yeah. Next time I call answer the phone."

There was another shout from the front hall. It sounded like Sy Koller.

"I'll answer the phone."

"Nice talking with you," Roz Nachman said. "Maybe sometime I'll come down."

"You might as well," Fletch said. "Everyone else has."

"I'll kill you!"

Fletch hurried through the billiard room and along the corridor to the front hall.

Sy Koller stood halfway down the stairs, facing downward.

Gerry Littleford stood just below him on the stairs, facing upward. He was naked. In his right hand was a carving knife.

Gerry was sexually aroused. Every muscle in his

137

lean body was taut. His skin shone with sweat. He was moving like a panther about to pounce.

He was beautiful.

Koller took a step backward, up the stairs.

"What are you all doing to me?" Gerry asked, softly.

"Gerry, you've been working hard," Koller said. "There's been strain."

At the top of the stairs, leaning on the bannister, Geoff McKensie watched. Something in his eyes was turning over like a reel of film.

On the floor of the front hall were Gerry's red bikini underpants.

"No, no," said Gerry. "I's not that. I know it's not that. I'm black. You all think I'm black."

Koller laughed nervously. "Gerry, you are black."

Gerry plunged the knife at Koller's fat, white legs. Koller jumped up another step. His face was wet with sweat, too.

Mrs Lopez was in the diningroom door. "He's got my knife," she said to Fletch.

"Say *man*, Sy. Go ahead. Say *man*. Say *boy*."

"I never called you *boy* in my life. I never would."

Gerry lunged again. Koller stepped sideways on the stair.

"You're insulting me," said Koller.

"I'm a twenty-seven-year-old professional actor!" Gerry screamed.

"Good one, too," Koller said mildly.

"I'm a *man*!"

"Gerry, that's obvious. If you'd just put down the knife. Give it to Fletcher..."

"Gerry," Fletch said quietly. "This is not a good day for you to be threatening someone with a knife. It doesn't look good. You know what I mean?"

Gerry pivoted on the stair to look down at Fletch fully.

"Don't call me *boy*."

"Who called you *boy*?"

Mrs Lopez said, "That's my good knife."

Sy Koller laughed. "Come on, Gerry. You can't expect to be asked to play *Robin Hood of Sherwood Forest*."

."Everyone's always beatin' up on me," Gerry said.

"That's in the movies, Gerry," Sy Koller said. "You're a well-paid professional actor. At home you drive a Porsche. No one beats you up."

"Goddamn it!" He slashed at Sy Koller's legs.

Koller jumped back, up another stair. His green T-shirt flapped.

Fletch heard Moxie walk along the upper corridor. She, or something like her, appeared at the top of the stairs. They were her legs between white shorts and white sneakers. The torso was her's, in a light blue sport shirt. The head was wrapped in a red kerchief. The face was matted with rouge and powder. Bright red lipstick enlarged her mouth ridiculously. The eyes were covered by giant sunglasses in white plastic frames.

Koller said, as if threatening, "Gerry, I'm not going to jump another stair."

"Oh, for goodness' sake." Moxie started down the stairs.

"Be careful," Fletch said.

She passed Koller and stood on the stair with Gerry. She ignored the knife. She took his erect penis in her hand and shook it as if she were shaking hands. "You need something else to think about, boy."

"You called him *boy*," Koller said. "She called him *boy*."

"I should call him girl?" asked Moxie. "With his prick in my hand?"

Mrs Lopez climbed the steps, reached around Gerry, and took the knife from his hand. "My good knife," she said. She started back to the kitchen.

"Get Mrs Littleford, will you?" Fletch asked Mrs Lopez.

"They're all against me." Gerry confided to Moxie. "You should see what they're doin' to me."

Moxie put her hands on his wet, shining shoulders. "It's just the coke, honey. No one's doing anything to you. Everything's fine. You're fine. It's a nice day."

"It's not the coke. It's what they're doin' to me."

"It's that little white powder you keep puttin' up your nose, sweetheart," Moxie said. "Drugs do funny things to your mind. Have you heard that?"

Gerry was studying Sy Koller's legs. They were unscratched.

Stella came into the front hall. She had a bath towel in her hands.

"Gerry needs an airing," Fletch said to her. "Why don't you walk him any direction from here until you come to water. And throw him in. He needs a swim." Her eyes had heavy lids. "You need a swim, too."

"I'm the one who needs the airing," Moxie said to Fletch. "Get me out of here."

"Dressed like that? You'll attract flies."

"No one will look at me," Moxie said.

"You're kidding."

On the stairs Stella was wiping down Gerry's whole body with the towel.

Looking at them, Fletch said, "Maybe a swim isn't a good idea."

"Who cares?" Moxie took Fletch by the hand.

"Don't swim out too far," Fletch said to Stella and Gerry.

He pulled Moxie sideways a moment and looked into the living room.

Edith Howell and Frederick Mooney were together on a Victorian loveseat. She had a gin and tonic in hand. His drink was in a short brandy glass.

"Revivals," Mooney was opining, "are anti-progress. Been far too many of 'em, lately. We must get ourselves out of the way, and let the young people create anew."

"But, Freddy," Edith said, *Time, Gentleman, Time* was a great musical. It still is."

"Come on." Fletch tugged Moxie's hand. "We'll go see the sunset. Out the back way. Through the Lopezes' yard."

17

"So," Fletch said. They were walking along White-head Street. Moxie's beautified head made Fletch feel he was walking along with a gift-wrapped package on a stick. "Gerry Littleford's mind runs to stabbing people with knives."

"That was nothing," Moxie said. "Forget about it."

"Your usual domestic incident? I thought things were getting rather serious there."

"You should never believe an actor," Moxie said. "It's not what's said that counts. It's the delivery."

"Including what you just said."

"I am lying, the liar said," Moxie said. "I wish he wouldn't use that stuff all the time."

"You mean you wish he would use it some of the time?"

"Sure. When he has an angry scene to play. He can become really frightening on the stuff."

"I saw that. But that's not acting, is it? I mean, it's just reacting to a drug."

"Acting is a drug, Fletcher. All art is. A distortion of perspective. A heightening of concentration. But when Gerry's just doing an ordinary hard scene the stuff works against him. Sets his timing off. Makes him overact."

"Do you use that stuff, Moxie? Like, for an 'angry scene'?"

"'Course not. I'm a better actor than Gerry." She looked across the street, at the big sign on the brick wall. "Wish I could go in there," she said. "I'd love to see Hemingway's bedroom. Also the room where he wrote. That was cute, what we did when we were playing pool. You have a good enough memory to be an actor."

"Moxie, do you think there are different rules for creative people?"

"Sure. There have to be special rules for being that alone."

"Something your father said this afternoon. Something about the obligations of talent being primary. We were talking about his relationship with you, and your mother, I guess. He said: 'Many men can love a woman and have a child; only a few can love the world and create miracles'."

"Dear O.L. Always the pretty turn of phrase." She walked in silence a moment. "I guess he's right."

"How can there be different rules for different people?"

"You just said it yourself, Fletch. I just said it. At the house you just said I couldn't go out—it wouldn't be safe. I just said I wished I could tour Hemingway's house. I wish I would be one hundred percent efficient as a creative person and one hundred percent efficient as a business person. I wish I didn't have to have a Steve Peterman living many of the normal aspects of my life for me." She turned him sideways on the sidewalk. "Look at me."

"I can't." He put his free hand over his eyes to shield himself from the sight of the kilograms of rouge, powder, lipstick, those foolish huge sunglasses on her face. "It's too 'orrible."

"I'm standing on a street in Key West," she said. "A marvelous live and let-live town. But, if you observe closely, I have to stand here observing different rules."

"There's been a murder."

He walked forward again.

"Sure." She walked with him. "If Jane Jones were involved in a murder, she could walk down the street without disguising herself as Miss Piggy. I can't." Crossing a sidestreet, the sun was warm on his face. "It's a question of energies, really," Moxie said. "Where do creative energies come from? If one has them, how does one best use them? When they wear down, how does one refurbish them? It's a joyous problem. It's also a responsibility, you see, all by itself. An extra responsibility. I guess, as Freddy says, a primary responsibility. And one just can't be totally responsible for everything. Few chefs take out the garbage. The day just isn't that long. No one's energies are that great."

Hand in hand, they walked through the long shadows of the palm trees on Whitehead Street.

After a while she dropped her hand.

"I know what your question is," she said in a low voice. "Your question is: do different rules for creative people give them the right to commit murder?"

"Don't cry," Fletch said. "It will make gulleys in your face powder."

"I did not murder Steve Peterman," Moxie said. "It's important that you believe me, Fletch."

Fletch said, "I know."

"Wow!" Moxie said. "What's all this about?"

"Sunset."

There were hundreds of people on the dock. Spaced to keep out of each other's sounds, there was a rock band, a country band, a string ensemble. There was a juggler juggling oranges and an acrobatic team bouncing each other into the air. There was a man dressed as Charlie Chaplin doing the funny walk through the crowd. There was an earnest young man preaching The Word of The Lord and a more earnest young man in a brown shirt and swastika armband preaching racial discrimination, and a most earnest young man satirizing them both, exhorting the people to believe in canned peas. Each had an audience of listeners, watchers, cheerers, and jeerers.

Across the water, the big red sun was dropping slowly to the Gulf of Mexico.

The people milling around on the dock, ambling from group to group, looking at each other, listening to each other, taking pictures of each other, were of every sort extant. One hundred miles of Florida Keys hang from continental U.S.A., like an udder, and to the southernmost point drip the cream and the milk and the scum of the whole continent. There are the artists, the writers, the musicians, young and old, the arrived, the arriving, and the never-to-arrive. There are numbers of single people of all ages, sometimes in groups, the searchers who sometimes find. There are the American families, with children and without, the professional and the working class, the retired and the honeymooners. There are the drug victims and the drug smugglers, the filthy, mind blown, and the gold-bedecked, corrupt, corrupting despoilers of the human being.

"Wow," said Moxie. "What a fashion show."

The people there were dressed in tatters and tailor-made, suits and strings, rags and royal gems.

"You should talk," Fletch said, grinning into her huge plastic glasses.

"So many people for a sunset."

"Happens every night. Even cloudy nights."

"What an event. Someone should sell tickets. Really. Think what you have to do to get this many people into a theater."

After touring the crowd, listening to the music, watching the performers, Fletch and Moxie found an empty place on the edge of the dock and sat down. Their legs dangled over the water.

"What an outer reality," Moxie said.

"Which reminds me," Fletch said. "Simple enough question: who is the producer of *Midsummer Night's Madness*?"

"Steve Peterman."

"I thought you said he was executive producer, or something."

"He is. Sort of. There is another producer, Talcott Cross. I never met him. His job is finished, for now. He worked at setting things up. Casting. Most of the location work. You know, hiring people."

"Where is he?"

"Los Angeles, I suppose. I think he lives in Hollywood Hills. Steve intended to be the line-producer on this film. That is, stay with it during shooting, and all that."

"So which of them hired Geoff McKensie and which hired Sy Koller?"

"Cross hired McKensie. Peterman fired him."

"And Peterman hired Koller."

"Right."

"So Peterman is more powerful than Cross? I mean, one of the co-producers is more equal than the other?"

"Sure. Cross is more of an employee. Hired to do the production stuff Steve didn't want to do, or didn't have time to do."

"Does Cross get a share of the profits?"

"I suppose so. But probably not as big a share as Steve . . . would have gotten."

Down the dock, also sitting on the edge, a girl in cut-off jeans was staring at Moxie.

"What makes Steve Peterman as a producer more powerful than his co-producer, what's-his-name Cross?"

"Talcott Cross. Everything in this business, Fletch, comes down to one word: the bank. Where the money comes from."

"Okay. That's my question. I thought a producer was someone who raises money for a film."

"A producer does an awful lot more than that."

The girl in cut-off blue jeans nudged the boy sitting next to her. She said something to him.

"But it was Steve Peterman who raised the money for this film."

"Yes. From Jumping Cow Productions, Inc."

"What's that?"

"An independent film company. A company set up to invest in films. The world's full of 'em."

"Forgive me for never having heard of it. Has it made many films?"

"I don't think so. I think it has some others in pre-production. Most likely it has. I don't know, Fletch. It could be a bunch of dentists who have pooled their money to invest in movies. Jumping Cow Productions could be a subsidiary of International Telephone and Telegraph, for all I know."

Half the big red sun had sizzled into the Gulf. A black, ancient-rigged sloop was sailing up the harbor toward them.

"Don't you care who's producing your film?" Up the dock-edge Moxie was causing widening interest among the group of young people. "I mean, if the source of the money is so all-fire important..."

Moxie sighed. "Steve Peterman was producing this film."

The top of the sun bubbled on the horizon and was extinguished.

In the harbor, in front of the dock, the Sloop *Providence* fired her cannon and ran down the stars and stripes prettily.

And the people on the dock cheered.

Evening in Key West had been declared.

Fletch swung his feet onto the dock and stood up. "Let's go home."

"But, Fletch, after the sunset is better than before. That's when the clouds pick up their colors."

"There aren't any clouds."

She looked at the sky. "You're right."

The young people down the dock had stood up, too.

"Come on," Fletch said. "We can walk slowly. Look back." Moxie got to her feet. "You see the sun set in the ocean all the time anyway," he said.

The girl in cut-offs was facing Moxie. "I know what you're trying to do," the girl said.

Her friends were all around her.

Moxie said nothing. She stepped closer to Fletch and took his arm.

"You're trying to look like Moxie Mooney," the girl laughed.

Moxie said, "Actually, I'm not."

The young people around the girl laughed. One said, "Oh yeah."

The girl said, "Moxie doesn't wear all that crap on her face."

"She doesn't?" Moxie asked.

"She's natural," the girl said. "She don't wear no make-up at all."

"You've seen her?"

"Naw. But she's stayin' somewhere here in Key West."

"She's over on Stock Island," said the boy. "In seclusion."

"Yeah," said another boy. "She murdered somebody."

Moxie's arm flexed against Fletch.

"You really think Moxie Mooney killed somebody?" she asked.

"Why not?" shrugged a boy.

"What are you—a look-alike contest?" asked another girl.

"I want to see her," the girl in cut-offs said. "I'm gonna see her."

"Well," Fletch said. He tugged Moxie's arm. "Good luck."

The girl in cut-offs called after Moxie. "You look sorta like her."

"Thanks," Moxie called back. Miserably, she said, "I guess."

They were walking back on Whitehead Street. There was some color in the sky.

"Anyway," Fletch said in a cheery tone, "I enjoyed talking with your father this afternoon."

"You like him, don't you."

"I admire him," Fletch said. "Enormously."

150

"I guess he's a brilliant man," Moxie admitted. "He's funny."

"After all these decades of acting," Moxie said, "he speaks as if every line were written for him. He says *Good Morning* and you have to believe it's a good morning—as if nobody had ever said it before."

"How come he's all-of-a-sudden so attentive to you?"

"He's not. He just landed on me. Can't find work, I guess. Nobody else wants him."

"Did he call you, did he write you, did he arrange to stay with you?"

"Course not. He had taken up residence in my apartment in New York. I didn't even know it. When I went there a few weeks ago—you know, to talk to Steve Peterman—there he was at home in my apartment. His clothes and his bottles all over the place. He was nearly unconscious. Looking at cartoons on the television. I had to put him to bed."

"Jesus," Fletch said. "Frederick Mooney looking at cartoons on television. All the bad satires of himself."

"I was pretty upset anyway. Yelling into the phone, trying to find Steve."

"Had you given him a key to the apartment?"

"No. He had never been there before."

"How did he get in?"

"The doorman gave him a key. He is Frederick Mooney, after all."

"I heard someone else say that."

"I mean, everyone knows he's my father. I had never told the doormen to keep him out. What

151

else could they do—have a legendary genius raving in their lobby?"

"Different rules," said Fletch. "This may seem strange to you, Moxie, put me down with those kids on the dock, but I'm proud and pleased to know your father. I find him damned interesting. I mean, for me to really see him and talk with him and know him. Even though he keeps confusing me with a corpse."

"You're not a corpse, Fletcher." Moxie stroked his arm. "Not yet, anyway. Of course, if you get me to sign any more papers in the dark..."

"Think of all he's done."

"I had to bring him down here with me. What else could I do with him? Couldn't leave him sitting there in New York."

"So you packed him up and poured him onto the plane."

"He entertained everybody in the first-class section. He had a few drinks, of course. There was a little girl, about twelve years old, sitting across the aisle from him. He started telling her the story of *Pygmalion*. He got everybody's attention by making all Eliza Doolittle's mouth noises. Began playing all the parts at once. Henry Higgins, the father. Then he began singing all the songs from *My Fair Lady*. People were standing in aisles. *Get me to the church, get me to the church, get me to the church on time*..." Moxie sawed out flat and guttural. "People crowded up from the coach section."

"Marvelous," Fletch said.

"It's nuts!" she exclaimed.

"Yeah, nuts. But the little girl will never forget

it. No one aboard will. Frederick Mooney doing Shaw at thirty thousand feet."

"Nuts!" she said. "Nuts! Nuts! Nuts!"

"I think it's nice."

"Against safety regulations," Moxie said. "Have that many people in the aisles. Utterly nuts."

"The obligations of talent," Fletch said. "Different rules."

"He's a drunk," Moxie said easily. "He's a mad, raving drunk."

"But you love him."

"Hell," she said. "I love him about as much as I love Los Angeles. He's just very big on my landscape."

18

Dinner at the Blue House was conch chowder, red snapper and Key lime pie. Mrs. Lopez provided the best Key West dining.

Before dinner, Lopez told Fletch Global Cable News had called several times and would like him to return the call. Fletch thanked him and did not return the call.

During dinner Frederick Mooney said to Moxie, *"But yet thou art my flesh, my blood, my daughter—or rather a disease that is in my flesh, which I must needs call mine."*

"Oh, no," Moxie said. "More Lear."

Edith Howell said, "Freddy's a *learing* old man."

"And you, Madame," said Frederick Mooney, "are a bag of wind."

And during dinner, Sy Koller said, "I knew something was going on between Dan Buckley and Steve Peterman. Buckley was not happy with Peterman..." He ran through his theory of the murder again, adding the idea this time that maybe Peterman had gotten Buckley into something illegal...

Moxie said nothing.

Stella Littleford, looking even smaller and more bedraggled than usual, said, "Marge Peterman." As she spoke, she kept giving sad glances at her husband, who, after his swim, was still acting a little jumpy and at first kept his smiles perfunctory and his conversation to the mannerly minimum. "Wives can get to the point," Stella said, "where divorce isn't adequate. How long had the Petermans been married—ten years? And this was the first time I've ever seen Marge Peterman with her husband. I didn't even know there was a Marge Peterman. And all this time Peterman's been runnin' all over the world, going to bed with people, doin' what he wanted..."

"I don't know," Fletch said. "Did Peterman jump in and out of bed with people, Moxie?"

"Steve was interested in only one thing," Moxie said, performing fine surgery on her fish. "Money. And talk, talk, talk, talk, talk. About money."

"A wife gets tired of gettin' shoved aside," Stella Littleford insisted. "Of everybody tellin' her she's not important. Of bein' told to do this, do that, do the other thing, and otherwise shut up and stay in the background. That could drive anybody to murder."

155

"Stella killed Peterman," giggled Gerry Littleford. "Out of respect for his wife."

Stella colored. "Okay," she said. "Why was Marge Peterman there? She'd never shown up before. There was no weekend planned, or anything. Our work schedule gave Peterman no more time off than it gave us. We had weeks to go before a break."

"Is what you're saying, Stella," Fletch asked. "Is that Marge Peterman showed up on location with the intention of killing her husband?"

"Sure."

"Does anybody know if she was expected?" Fletch looked around at the faces at his table.

"I don't think she was," Sy Koller said. "When you're on location, directors—at least some of us—prefer not to have wives around..." He looked quickly at Geoffrey McKensie and then away. "Extraneous people." He looked at Frederick Mooney who was blinking drunkenly over his plate. His eyes settled on Stella Littleford. "Apt to be damned distracting. It's tough enough, you know, dealing with the emotions, the feelings, of the people working on a film. When those people have wives around, and husbands around to back them up, echo everything they say: lovers, retainers, and the odd relative..." Again Koller glanced at Mooney. "All telling them they're right, they're wrong, they're this, they're that, they *look tired this morning*—" Koller's voice went to a bitchy falsetto, "—*and is that a pimple coming under your nose? And tell that Sy Koller that scene will never be right until he gives you a stronger exit line*... Makes it damned tough for the director." Sy Koller laughed at himself. "Didn't mean to take advantage of a simple question and climb on my hobby horse. No," he said to Fletch. "I don't think Marge Peterman was expected. I think Peterman and I were of one mind on this topic. I bribed my own wife off with a trip to Belgium. I think if Steve knew his wife was coming he could have asked her not to."

"And she would have stayed home in her closet," Stella said with disgust.

"Stroking her chinchilla," put in Edith Howell.

"Well, this time Marge Peterman didn't stay home," insisted Stella Littleford. "She showed up on location and stabbed the bastard."

Gerry snickered.

"Well, where was she during the taping of *The Dan Buckley Show*?" Stella asked.

"With me," Fletch answered.

"And who the hell are you?"

"Nobody."

"He's our host," said Edith Howell. "Would somebody please pass the wine?"

"And later," said Stella, "where was she? We found her over there behind those trailers."

"With me," Fletch said.

"Looked to me like she was hiding," said Stella.

"It's decided." Gerry Littleford put down his knife and fork. "Stella killed Steve Peterman and thus struck another blow for the equality of women."

Mooney's eyes kept closing and his head kept bobbing and he kept eating. He was napping during dinner.

"Investors," said Geoff McKensie.

"Yeah," mocked Moxie. "Let's hear it from the investors."

McKensie wrinkled his eyebrows at her. Apparently, like most taciturn men, when McKensie spoke, he expected to be heard. He waited for attention and then spoke in a tone far friendlier than what he had to say to the people present: "I've been thinking it out. Who had the most reason to kill Steve Peterman? He was really muckin' this film up, he was. Here the company had hired a first class director—me. I only took on the job with the understandin' I could have a free hand with the script. I spent months goin' over that script. My wife and I flew halfway 'round this spinnin' earth. I spent a week in California, thrashing the new script out with Talcott Cross. He approved everything I wanted to do. 'Course, he's a professional, he is. I come out here to this American boot camp for heaven—"

"I think he means Florida," Fletch whispered to Moxie.

"—and here's this Peterman bloke rollin' 'round on his back like a pig turnin' everything on the menu into garbage."

Sy Koller's color was deepening. "You mean, he fired you."

"Right he did," said McKensie. "And he hires a second-rate, has-been director—" McKensie jerked his thumb at his directorial table mate. "—who proceeds to film the original lousy script as if it was half-good. As if it was any good."

"Excuse me for living," said Sy Koller. He was a deep crimson.

"Come on, Geoff," said Edith Howell. "Be fair. You were the victim of a terrible, terrible tragedy. Your wife was killed. You couldn't expect to carry on—"

"I'm not used to yankee-land," said McKensie. "With a little luck, I never will be, I now think. But where I come from—Down Under—when something like that happens a decent interval takes place. A chap's allowed to take the blow and recover."

"Come on, McKensie," Gerry Littleford said. "You were in no shape to direct after your wife's death. You still aren't. How could you be?"

McKensie's eyes attacked Littleford. "I'll tell you, sonny, your best chance was to film my script. With me directing." He made another disparaging gesture toward Koller. "You haven't got a lawyer's chance in heaven doin' things they way you're doin' 'em."

Fletch was looking at Moxie. His eyes were repeating, *Having two directors in the house is like having two ladies wearing the same expensive dress.*

"What happened here?" McKensie asked rhetorically, dropping his h's onto his plate. "The day after my wife was killed there was no filming— of course. That same damn day this failed director—" Again, he jerked his thumb at Koller. "—is flown in by Steven Peterman. Named the director of *Midsummer Night's Madness.* My script is thrown into the hopper and the day after that, you all start filming the original pile of garbage. He didn't even wait until after the funeral."

"I know, Geoff, " Moxie said. "I spoke to Steve

about that. I thought it was rotten. I tried to get him to hold off filming for a few days—"

"It wasn't respectful, for one thing," said McKensie. "My wife was a lady who deserved a little respect, you know."

"I'm sure she was," Edith Howell said quickly. "I wish we had all known her."

"But Steve said," continued Moxie. "Oh, you know what he said. He said, how many thousands of dollars filming costs a day. How many thousands of dollars it cost to have the whole crew idle."

"'Idle'," scoffed McKensie. "Respect for the dead, I'd call it. A little respect for the bereaved."

"Steve read me the figures," Moxie said. "Said the investors would have every reason to raise hell if we closed down for a few days."

"Exactly," McKensie said. "Investors. Maybe your investors have got more sense than Peterman gave 'em credit for. Maybe in the old days in Hollywood you could pull the line *investors don't want the movie good—they want it Thursday*. But films cost a bit too much for that, these days. From my experience with investors, they'd rather have a piece of somethin' that has a chance of makin' a profit than a piece of somethin' that stinks so bad it'll have to be buried at sea."

Koller's face was going through the whole color spectrum. "Tell me, McKensie," he said. "If you think *Misdummer Night's Madness* is basically such a lousy script, how come you agreed to direct it in the first place?"

160

"You don't expect me to be honest about that, do you?" McKensie said.

Koller raised and dropped his hands in despair. "Right now, I don't know what to expect."

"It was my chance to direct in America," Geoffrey McKensie said. "I thought I could make a silk slipper out of a dog's paw. I could have, too." He sat back on his chair. Lopez was clearing the table. "If I were an investor in *Midsummer Night's Madness,* and I knew what was going on on location, I would have murdered Steve Peterman ruddy fast. The bastard deserved it."

"But there was no one on location, Geoff," Gerry Littleford said, "except those of us actively making the film. The location had been secured."

"Bullsdroppings," said McKensie. "At that moment, there were several alleged members of the press on location. You can't tell me one of them couldn't have been a kill artist."

"Me again," said Fletch.

"You," said McKensie. "You're a member of the press? I haven't been able to find a typewriter anywhere in this house. I spent the afternoon lookin'. In your own room, there isn't a pad of paper, or a pencil, a camera..."

"Good point," said Fletch.

"What the hell were you doin' on location then?" McKensie asked.

"I admit," said Fletch, "getting on location wasn't that difficult. I expect anybody who really wanted to, could have. But... they'd have to show some identification."

Finally, Koller's cholera caroomed. "McKensie," he said, "you're full of down-under dung. So far you've made three small—very small—films, somewhere in the Outback, a million miles from nowhere, no pressure on you, with all the time in the world. Artsy-smartsy films. For God's sake, they haven't even really been released outside Australia. Your world-wide audience would fit into a mini-bus. And everyone in the back seat would only pretend to understand what you're tryin' to do. And suddenly you're God Almighty. The *Grand Auteur*. Listen to me, babe—I've made more films that you've ever seen. You know how many films I've made? Thirty eight! Okay, so the last five didn't do so well. Three is all you've made, buster! Hell, my wife knows more about directing than you'll ever know, just from listenin' to me talk. And I've made better films than you'll ever make. Damn it all, at least when I film night scenes like in *Midsummer Night's Madness,* I give the audience enough light to see what's goin' on. You make that film and the last third of the picture would be so dark, the audience wouldn't even be able to find their way out of their seats to go home." Koller took a deep breath. "Just because some of us are courteous to you, kid, don't think you're such a hotshot."

McKensie didn't seem too disturbed by this laceration. He was eating his lime pie.

"Well," Edith Howell said into the thick silence, "where did John Meade go? Fletch, you said he was just doing an errand."

"He is. Just ran up to New York for a minute."

"New York?" exclaimed Edith. "For a minute? We're two thousand miles from New York, aren't we?"

"Just for a minute," Fletch said. "Doing an errand for Moxie. He'll be back tonight. John said he'd do anything in the world for Moxie."

"Mister McKensie," boomed Mooney in what doubtlessly was meant to be taken as a proper manner. "Mister Peterkin tells me you are about to commence principal photography on a film of William Shakespeare's *Midsummer Night's Dream*."

Everyone at table looked at everyone else.

"O.L.," Moxie said gently.

"If so," continued Mooney, now obviously addressing Sy Koller, "I should very much like to be considered for a part, however small..."

Gerry Littleford giggled.

"Not Oberon, of course," conceded Mooney, "bit too thick in the leg for that these days. But you might consider me for Theseus, you know. I've played it before, and I've always thought Philostrate a smashing role."

"Really, O.L. Stop it."

"Well, daughter, no one else seems to want to have me, these days. Of course, my managers rather ran up the price of my talents these last few years. I wouldn't pay myself what people have had to pay me. I'm sure all that salary-fee business can be adjusted, for a small role. Mister McKensie—" Frederick Mooney smiled at Sy Koller. "—you're in luck, as you've caught me between engagements, as it were."

163

"Goddamn it!" Moxie exploded. "Why don't you consider yourself retired?" She pushed her chair back from the table. "Superannuated? Shelved? Out to pasture?"

"Moxie?" Fletch said.

She stood up, nearly knocking her chair over. "Why don't you think of joining mother in the asylum? You put her there. You've put yourself there. Why don't you go?"

Moxie left the dining room.

"Her exits are getting better as the day goes on," Stella commented. "I can hardly wait to see how dramatically she goes to bed."

"She didn't even slam a door that time," Gerry said.

"That was good." Sy Koller looked at where she had been sitting. "She created all the effect of a slammed door without slamming a door. All the effect of knocking over her chair without knocking it over."

"What are you guys talking about?" asked Fletch. "There is no door."

"There's always a door," said Sy Koller, "in your mind."

"I have embarrassed my daughter," uttered Frederick Mooney remorsefully. "She resists thinking of me as a bit player. She forgets, or she never knew, all the small things I have had to do...in this business, to keep afloat."

"Coffee, anyone?" Fletch asked. Lopez had appeared with a pot.

"Global Cable News called again," Lopez said

while pouring out Fletch's coffee. "A Mister Fennelli. I said I'd give you the message."

"Thank you." Fletch smiled at those remaining at table. "At the moment, I don't think I have anything to report."

19

After dinner, Fletch found Geoffrey McKensie in the billiard room playing alone.

Fletch chose a cue stick and McKensie triangled the balls.

They played almost through a game without saying anything.

Finally, McKensie said, "Sorry. 'Fraid I behaved pretty badly at dinner. I ran on like a young lady not invited to the garden party."

"Not to worry," Fletch said. "You had some things that needed saying and you said 'em."

Continuing in the tone of one vexed with himself, McKensie clucked, "What will you Yanks think of us Aussies."

"Us Yanks will think of you Aussies as lovingly

as we always have." At Fletch's stroke, the cue ball neatly avoided every other ball on the table.

McKensie sank two and took his third shot.

"Good at sports, too," Fletch said. "Damn it." He bounced the cue ball off several, leaving McKensie with a wonderful lay. "Tell me, though—those things you said—were you saying them because you really believe someone in Jumping Cow Productions might really have been gunning for Peterman—or were you just saying them to dump on Koller?"

McKensie took a careful shot and sank two at once.

Fletch hung up his stick.

"I don't know," McKensie said. "It's true—Koller was a good director—back before he sank his integrity in the briney. Nowadays, it doesn't bother him to shoot a bad script—as long as he gets paid for it. What hurts is that he knows better. It's also true that Peterman was mucking things up royally. He deserved the cold steel between his ribs."

Seeing Fletch had quit, McKensie resumed playing by himself and cleaned off the table.

Fletch asked, "Do you think Peterman could have been sabotaging this film on purpose?"

"I can't think of a reason. Nobody likes to lose money." McKensie hung up his own cue. "But I'll tell you, Peterman couldn't have done more to torpedo that film if he were doin' it deliberate."

"Drink?" Fletch asked. "There's some bad American beer."

"Brought some scripts with me from home," McKensie said. "Think I'll go do some work on 'em. Somethin' tells me Koller won't want to continue talkin' shop with me this night."

20

Outside in the dark, Edith Howell and Sy Koller were sitting in the comfortable chairs on the cistern sipping large Scotches.

"Do you know," Edith Howell said to Fletch as he sat down with them, "that Freddy has escaped the premises again?"

"Key West is a good place to go out."

"He's like a cat. When you think he's in he's out and out in."

"Gone out for conviviality," Fletch said. "Do you worry about him?"

"Freddy? Good God, no. He has millions."

Fletch swallowed what to him was a *non sequitur.* "Of dollars?"

"Tens of millions. I know that for a fact."

Fletch shook his head. "Somehow, I thought he was broke. I think Moxie thinks he's broke."

"Tens of millions," repeated Edith Howell. "I know of what I speak. I have friends whose friends are friends of Freddy, if you know what I mean. He has millions all over the world, just lying around."

"Pity you can't get your grubby fingers on it all, Edith," Sy Koller said.

"I'm tryin', darlin', I'm tryin'. Did you hear him in there asking the world for a bit part in a movie that's not even being made? The poor dear. He needs looking after."

"He's as crazy as a mosquito in the dressing room of a chorus line," said Sy Koller. "Gonzo."

"It's interesting to know him," Fletch said.

"That's because you don't," said Edith Howell. "Knowing Freddy is like having a rare disease: shortly the interest pales and what's left is pain."

Sy Koller laughed. "Apparently you're willing to put up with the pain, Edith. For all those millions."

"For a short while, darling. After all, Freddy's liver can hardly be made of molybdenum."

21

"Well, darlings." Edith Howell picked up her drink and stood up. "If you're not chatting you might as well be dead, I always say. Or asleep." Sitting out in the night, she and Sy Koller and Fletch had been silent for two minutes. "So I might as well go to bed."

After she closed the door to the house behind her, Sy Koller lifted his drink to Fletch and said, "I like my drink, too, you see."

"You've had a hard day," Fletch said. "Attacked with a knife by one of your actors. Orally attacked by one of your colleagues."

"Ah, the perils of being a director." Sy Koller chuckled. "Being a director is like being the father of a large family of berserk children who keep slipping in and out of reality. We get paid for hazardous duty, but not enough."

"I thought I should tell you," Fletch said slowly, "that the police know that you and Peterman had a fist fight outside a Los Angeles restaurant three years ago."

"They do? How do you know that?"

"Talked to Chief of Detectives Roz Nachman this afternoon. She called. She accused me of having hijacked all her prime suspects."

"I'm a prime suspect?" Koller ran his palm over his stubbly chin and cheeks. "I shouldn't be."

"No?"

"Why should I put myself out of a job? Now that Peterman's dead the future of *Midsummer Night's Madness* is dubious."

"You mean you won't even finish filming it?"

"Well," Koller snorted. "Peterman was the only one who seemed to believe in the property."

"Didn't you believe in it?"

"Not really. Peterman gave me the script and said he wanted it shot exactly as written."

"You never even saw McKensie's script?"

"No. Peterman said it was a pile of dung."

"Do you think it would have been?"

"Probably not. But it was clear to me that McKensie had every reason in the world to sue Peterman, so how could I ask to use his script? It would confuse matters. You don't know this business, do you?"

"No."

"Think of having a career where you have to find a whole new job every six months."

"Finding a job is the hardest job there is."

"That's the director's life. And the actor's life. And the set designer's. It brings a certain element of the frantic to this business. And a great deal of hot air."

"But don't you get rich and famous after a while? Able to pick and choose?"

"Seldom. You make a pile of money, and you spend a pile and a half. Because you're so frantic. You blow it on hot air, keeping up the image. The more money you make the more frantic you become, the more you blow it on hot air and the deeper into debt you go, which makes you more frantic."

In the trees night birds were gossiping.

"Anyway, the police say you were fighting over a woman."

"Is that what they say? I guess it's what we said at the time."

"That you had Peterman down on the sidewalk and were strangling him when you were pulled off."

"Yeah," Koller sighed. "It felt good."

Fletch said: "She must have been one fantastical woman."

"I wish I'd ever known a woman worth strangling someone over." Koller lit a cigarette. "Methinks, mine host, you enquire as to why I was strangling Steve Peterman."

"Just curious," said Fletch. "Did he stick you with one of his telephone bills?"

Koller took a drink. "Happy to tell you. Because my strangling Steve Peterman three years ago is the best evidence I've got that I didn't stab him yesterday."

Fletch waited. The tip of Koller's cigarette glowed brightly.

"I caught him out in a fraud," Koller said. "I resented it. I hated it. Peterman wasn't the first to work this scam, and he wasn't the last. But, Fletcher, this business can be so dirty...sometimes it gets to you. What he was doing was raising money for a film which didn't exist, and never would. He had gotten ahold of something which looked like a filmscript, a story about some South American *patron* and his daughter and a priest and a revolutionary—a complete mess. Anybody who knew anything about the business would know it wasn't a filmscript. It was just a hundred pages of people saying hello and goodbye and making speeches at each other. He had been out peddling this to people who didn't know better across this broad land—you know, the doctors and the shoemakers, the widows and the orphans, all who dream of making a financial killing on a big movie while having their lives touched with glamor. They'd be invited to the opening in New York. Also the Academy Award ceremony of course. He told the suckers he just wanted start-up money, to be paid back when and if he got the film capitalized."

"But not to be paid back if he did not get the film capitalized?"

"Of course not. Told them it was going to be filmed in El Salvador. Even had an El Salvadorean S. A. Had no intention of trying to capitalize it. You never heard of this scam?"

"No."

"I figure he'd raised about a half million dollars, all of which had disappeared down this El Salvadorean hole." Koller stubbed out his cigarette. "I hated this for two reasons. It's bad for the business. The next guy who goes out and tries to raise start-up money for a film might be honest. The more of these little cheats there are running around, the harder it is for the honest guy." Koller drank. "The second reason, of course, was that he was using my name. He had told these people maybe he could get Sy Koller to direct. That we'd had conversations. That we were in negotiations."

"Not true?"

"I'd never met the son of a bitch. First I'd heard about it was when Sonny Fields told me he'd heard it was going on." Koller lit another cigarette, his lighter flaring in the dark garden. "So, one night after more to drink than was good for me, I met Peterman in a Los Angeles bar, pulled him out to the sidewalk by his coat collar, proceeded to hit him upside the head. He fell to the sidewalk. I sat on top of him and proceeded to throttle him. It felt real good. His neck was soft. No muscle at all. Wonder I didn't kill him before nosey people interfered."

"Why didn't Peterman press charges?"

"Why didn't I have him arrested for fraud?"

"I don't know."

"We came to an amicable settlement. Peterman said he was just using this scam to raise money for a real film, somewhere down the road. My career wasn't looking too good. Aforementioned frantic need to gain employment. So..."

"So...?"

"I agreed that if he ever had a real film to direct, I would direct it. We laid the fight off on a woman."

"You blackmailed him."

"We blackmailed each other. It's the way much of this business works, old son."

"And what happened to the half a million dollars?"

"It went into Peterman's pockets. And then into his shoes and his wife's furs."

"So *Midsummer Night's Madness* came along, starring Moxie Mooney, whom Peterman by then controlled, and Gerry Littleford—"

"And Talcott Cross hires Geoffrey McKensie to direct. I called Steve Peterman."

"Had you seen the script?"

"No. But I had a pretty good idea it wasn't much good."

"Why would you want to direct a loser?"

"Well.... In the three intervening years my career had sunk so low I was getting the bends. You understand?"

"How would directing a stinker help your career?"

"It would prove I could get employed. It would also provide me with some much needed money. You know about money?"

"I'm learning."

"End of story," said Koller. "As long as Peterman was producing, Koller was directing. Peterman dead: Koller dead. *Ergo* the one person absolutely guaranteed not to kill Steven Peterman is your's truly. Maybe it's a shameful story," Koller concluded, "but it's a hell of an alibi."

"Fletch?" Moxie's voice came from the upper balcony of the Blue House. "Are you out there?"

"Yo." He stepped under the balcony.

She said, "If you give me any of that Romeo crap, I'll spit on your head."

"If only your fans could hear you now."

"Go find Freddy for me, will you? I was sort of rough on him."

"Yes, you were."

"If I want criticism," she said irritably, "I'll ask for it."

"You're asking for it."

22

After a long silence, while Fletch waited, the man's voice drawled over the phone, "Sorry. Chief Nachman says she can't come to the phone now."

"Please," said Fletch, with as much dignity as he could enlist. "Tell her it's her earwig calling."

"Earwig? You mean that little no-see-'um bug?"

"Right." Alone in the study at the back of The Blue House Fletch smiled. "Earwig."

There was another long silence before Chief of Detectives Roz Nachman picked up. "Yes, Fletcher?"

"Thank you for answering, Chief. You're working late."

"Has one of your house guests become overwhelmed with remorse and confessed to murder?"

"It's a classier crime than that."

"I know it is."

"I have a line of investigation for you, though. Just a suggestion, really."

"Suggest away."

"Steve Peterman must have had some kind of a car. A rented car or something. Everyone was up and down that Route 41 so much, between the two beaches."

"I suppose so."

"I suggest you check Peterman's car to see if it's been in an accident. A hit-and-run accident."

Nachman did not pause long. "You talking about McKensie's wife?"

"Just a thought. Wouldn't take much to check it out."

"I see."

"For what it's worth," Fletch said.

"All right."

"Is there still nothing showing up on all that film?"

"Nothing."

"And the experts aren't discovering anything funny about the set?"

"Nothing."

"That's a real significant fact in itself."

"Good night, Irwin. I'm busy."

23

The inside, the bar area of Durty Harry's, was virtually empty, but there was a huge crowd sitting and standing on the patio, all facing into the same corner.

Fletch got a beer from the bar and went out to the patio.

Quite a diverse collection of people had gathered. There were the tourists in the best light colored clothing one can really only buy in a big city but never really wear in one. Their faces and arms and legs were red and stiff with sunburn. There were the genuine denizens of Key West, the Conchs, who prefer to keep themselves as pale as Scandanavians in deep Scandanavian winters. They think of the sun as enemy, and run through it from building to car and car to house. There were some art-folk of all ages, their faces and bodies looking as if they'd lived plenty, their bright, quick eyes showing they wanted to live plenty more. There were the cocaine cowboys in their stringy leather and denim; the girls in their full skirts and full blouses and dead hair. And there were the drunks, with the weird blue in their skin which results from mixing too much constant alcohol with too much constant sun.

And sitting in the corner, the object of everyone's attention, sat and spoke Frederick Mooney. With his gray hair, stubble of beard, broad face and big eyes, he easily could have been the reincarnation of the person whom the people in Key West would most like to see reincarnated—Ernest Hemingway. Mooney was Papa, all right, and these were his children gathered around him.

Sipping his beer, Fletch leaned against the door jamb and listened.

"...not glorious, not glamorous at all," Mooney was saying. "Anyone who thinks so knows nothing. Anyone who thinks acting is simply a matter of popping the eyes in surprise..." Mooney popped his eyes in surprise at the crowd; there was a titter of admiration. "...of doing a double-take..." Mooney did a doubletake; the people laughed. ..."quivering the chin..." Mooney's chin quivered apparently uncontrollably; the people laughed harder. "...to weep..." Tears swelled in Mooney's eyes and dribbled down his cheeks; the people applauded. "...don't know what acting is." The virtuoso wiped his instrument dry and thrust it forward at his audience. "An actor must learn his craft. And his skill is not just in learning to control every muscle of his face. Not just in learning how to set his shoulders expressively. Not just in learning that how he places his feet—even when they are out of sight, off-camera—invariably is more important than anything he does with his face, because how you place your feet, how you balance yourself, how you posture yourself says more about who you are, your attitudes than anything else."

Sitting back in his chair in the attitude of a grandfather at the end of a full meal, Mooney reached for the bottle of cognac on the table, brought it to his lips, and took a good-sized swallow. "Thirsty work, this." He anticipated a burp, worked it up from his innards, gave full sound to it. He blinked and smiled in happy relief at his audience, and they applauded.

"The craft, the skills," Mooney said. "Barrymore once said, he'd rather have straight legs than know how to act. Of course, Barrymore had straight legs." He paused to allow his audience to laugh, and they did. "An actor must learn how to move in his clothes. You know that a man moves differently in a toga than he does in blue jeans... than he does in medieval hose...than he does in black tie. But do you know an actor must learn these skills? Even if an actor does not smoke those dirty weeds..." Disdainfully, Frederick Mooney waved his hand at a woman smoking a cigarette, "...he must learn to handle a cigarette as if he were addicted. One handles a cigarette differently than one handles a cigar. Few actors are, in themselves, violent people. No acting schools I've heard of have pistol firing ranges. Yet when an actor handles a gun, he must have learned to do so... so naturally that the gun seems an extention of his hand—not something strange and foreign to him, but something so much a part of his being, so necessary to his mental attitudes that the audience knows he can use it and will use it. My training was such, having been dragged up through the music halls of England and the carnivals of America as well, I not only learned the rhythms of Shakespeare, but how to handle a sword and fence with it as if my life depended upon it. I learned to ride a horse both like a Guardsman and an American Indian. John Wayne once said that he didn't know much about method acting, but he sure knew how to stop a horse on the mark. Of course, John Wayne could stop a horse on the mark." Again his audience chuckled. Looking at his audience, tying them all together by his gaze, Mooney saw Fletch. In his eyes there was only the barest flicker of recognition. He continued his lecture. "It may not seem it to you—oh, you who watch an actor act and think you can judge him, but who haven't the slightest knowledge or appreciation of the skills he employs to entertain you—but an actor must learn to ride a horse and a motorcycle, to use a rope, a lariat, to drink from a wine flagon, and open a bottle of champagne, to hold a violin, and to perform a right uppercut to the jaw—perfectly."

Mooney stopped talking. He moved his eyes over the surface of the small table before him like a farmer looking for first signs of a crop. He seemed to find no growth, and his look was sad.

Finally, sensing his lecture was over, the people began asking him questions.

Mister Mooney, how did you enjoy playing opposite Elizabeth Taylor?

What's the greatest role you've ever played?

Is it true you actually took heroin to play the jazz pianist in Keyboard?

Mooney folded his arms over the table and dropped his head. "Nothing's true," he muttered. "Nothing's true. It's all a lie."

Fletch worked forward through the crowd. He stepped over some people sitting on the floor.

What's your next picture going to be?

"Nothing's true."

You think you could ride a horse now, the state you're in?

Fletch picked up Mooney's flight bag. Mooney raised his head slowly and looked Fletch in the eye a long moment.

"Ah, Mister Paterson."

"Came to carry your bag," Fletch said.

"Kind of you." Widely, he pointed at the bottle on the table and at the bag. "That bottle goes in that bag," he said.

Fletch put the cork in the bottle and the bottle in the flight bag.

Did you really get malaria making Jungle Queen?

"Yes," Mooney answered, standing up, "and I've still got it."

You've just got the shakes, Mooney. The sweats.

Mooney stumbled a few times picking his way

184

through the crowd but never actually fell. Fletch did not hold onto him. At that moment, Mooney was far from being the graceful, competent person he was just describing, with all the skills of an actor.

The people who were most kind in getting out of his way, letting him pass, were those most apt to reach out to him, touch him, touch his clothes as he passed.

"I want to say good night to the dog," Mooney said to Fletch.

"Dog?"

"The black dog."

Again, when they were in the less congested bar area, Mooney said, "I really would like to say good night to that dog."

"I don't see a dog, Mister Mooney."

"Big, black dog," Mooney said. "Name of Emperor."

Fletch looked around. "I don't see any dog, Mister Mooney."

"He's on the other side of the bar," Mooney said.

"Why don't we go this way? It's quicker."

"All right." He smiled wonderfully at Fletch. "I've given that lecture ten thousand times," he said. "Know it as well as the ravings of *Richard III*. It's all nonsense, of course."

At the entrance to the alley, Mooney looked back into the bar. "A clean, well-lighted place," he said.

24

The phone rang and Fletch was off the bed and across the room answering it before he really knew what he was doing.

"Hello?"

"Fletch?" It was Martin Satterlee ready to dispense information.

"Good morning, Martin." Fletch sat in the chair next to the telephone table. "What time is it in New York?"

Through the windows to the balcony first light was in the sky.

"Five fifteen a.m."

"Then it must be here, too." Moxie was not in his bed. She had chosen to spend the night in a hammock on the balcony. "Find anything?"

"Not as much as we could have found if we hadn't been interrupted. An hour ago, the authorities swooped into Peterman's office, where we were working, and laid claim to all Ms. Mooney's financial records. Asked us politely but firmly to leave."

"They were quick. Did you show them Moxie's authorization?"

"Of course. It was not my scheme to be thought a burglar in the night. They had papers from a higher authority."

"Their piece of paper beat your piece of paper, huh?"

"Their piece of paper was signed by a judge. My piece of paper was signed by a movie star."

"So you're going to tell me everything is all right, and Moxie was just having a bad dream about all this..."

"Does *Yellow Orchid* mean anything to you, as a film title?"

"No."

"*In Ramon's Bed?*"

"No."

"*Twenty Minutes to Twelve?*"

"No, don't think so."

"*Midsummer Night's Madness?*"

"Of course. That's the film Moxie is making now."

"Are they actually making it?"

"I'm not sure. They have been."

"*Sculpture Garden?*"

"No."

"These are all films supposedly being made—I

should say, financed—by Jumping Cow Productions."

"Yes. All right."

"The sole proprietor of Jumping Cow Productions is Ms Marilyn Mooney."

"Holy Cow."

"Chief Executive Officer and Treasurer is, or was, Steven Peterman."

"Wave that in front of me again, Marty. Moxie owns Jumping Cow Productions?"

"One hundred percent."

"I know she doesn't know that. She keeps referring to Jumping Cow as 'them' and 'they.' In fact, I think she's been waiting word from someone at Jumping Cow as to whether filming on *Midsummer Night's Madness* is to continue."

"She's waiting to hear from herself."

"Wow."

"You can say she didn't know about it, Fletch, but her signature is in all the appropriate places. The Delaware incorporation papers, loan agreements—"

"Talk to me about the loan agreements, Marty."

"I wish I could tell you everything. I can't. Cops *interruptus*. We were able to discover there are huge sums of money floating around for no reason we were able to discover. Millions of dollars. Some of the monies seem to have been raised to produce these films—but we can't find any evidence that any of these films exist in any form whatsoever, except *Midsummer Night's Madness* which, by the way, seems to have a remarkably low budget. There are loans from Swiss banks and Columbian banks and Bolivian banks. Some of these loans seem to have been used to repay loans to banks in Honduras, Mexico, the Bahamas. Thoroughly confusing. On some loans, we couldn't find schedules of repayment, or that anything at all had been repaid. On other loans, which were being repaid, we couldn't find the pieces of paper which said the loans had actually been taken out in the first place."

Fletch had drawn his knees up and put his feet in the chair. He was warmer that way. "All this under the banner of Jumping Cow Productions?"

"No. A huge, huge amount of this activity is under her own name, personally."

"That's bad."

"I think so."

"Marty, how would you say she stands in general, financially, ahead or behind?"

"Haven't you been listening? Tons of money which exist on paper under her name, and under Jumping Cow Productions, Inc., don't seem to be anywhere."

"Stolen." .

"Disappeared."

"Then, financially, she is behind."

"I'd say so. If you were looking for a motive for murder, you found one. A big one."

"I wasn't, actually."

"I can't see how she can ever get out of trouble. No matter how young she is. Millions are missing. Of course, maybe if we had another three weeks with the books, we could find some of it."

"Can't she claim bankruptcy?"

"It's not just money I'm talking about, Fletch. A lot of baffling financial activity has been happening under her name. Again, I wasn't able to spend enough time with her financial records to use the word fraud advisedly—"

"Ow."

"And her tax filings have been negligent. I mean negligible. Negligent and negligible. Minimum filings, maximum extentions. There were I.R.S. pieces of paper among her records, but no real reportings of income, outgo, profit, loss."

"Jail."

"Well. For next year she shouldn't plan too big a New Year's Eve party."

"But she wasn't doing all that bad stuff. She didn't even know about it."

"It was going on under her name, and she signed things."

"Marty. What about her personal assets?"

"Well, she owns a cooperative apartment in New York—mortgaged to the maximum. Also a very expensive property in Malibu, California, also mortgaged to the maximum. Her ownership of common stock follows a very distinct pattern. She would purchase at fifty and sixty dollars a share and sell at twelve and sixteen dollars a share."

"Always?"

"Few exceptions."

"Tax losses? Do you think Peterman was trying to create tax losses?"

"He was creating losses, all right. Huge losses. No preferred stock, no bonds. And the companies in which she was invested were foreign companies no one ever heard of. I mean, like a chain of bakeries in Guatemala."

"Must be dough in that."

"A Mexican trucking company. A restaurant in Caracas, Venezuela."

"Caramba!"

"An unrelieved tale of woe, Fletch. The only other thing she seems to own in this country is half interest in a horse farm in Ocala, Florida."

"Oh."

"That mean something to you? Five Aces Farm."

"Oh." Fletch counted his toes. "The alleged owner of that farm, Ted Sills, was a friend of Peterman's. I guess. That is, I met Sills at a party at Moxie's apartment once in New York. Peterman introduced us."

"Well, your friend Moxie has paid for the shipment of an awful lot of race horses between here and Venezuela."

"Oh. But, Martin, Moxie didn't even recognize Ted Sills' name when I mentioned him yesterday. We're even staying in Ted Sills' house. Right now."

"Small world."

"Even I've invested in some of the son of a bitch's race horses."

"Maybe I should go through your papers, too."

"Maybe you should. Hell's bells, Marty, what does all this add up to?"

"I don't know. Wasn't able to spend that long with her papers. On the face of things, it looks like your Moxie Mooney had an excellent motive for killing Steven Peterman. The best. Not once, but several times."

"That's what the police will say, isn't it?"

"I expect so. Of course, they could always find a factor which makes everything come out all right. But I doubt it. Experience has taught me, Fletch, that honest people do not bury their honesty in dishonest-seeming records."

"Martin, is there anyway all this shifting of money about, taking loans, losing money could be thought to benefit Moxie?"

"I don't know."

"I mean, isn't it pretty clear from the papers she's the victim here?"

Martin Satterlee thought a short moment. "The presumption is, Fletch, that when a person goes in for sharp practices, he is doing so with some idea of personal benefit in mind."

"But, Marty, everything's such a mess!"

"People who go in for sharp practices usually make a mess. They usually lose. Losing, Fletch, is no evidence of virtue."

"Oh."

"I must also point out to you—seeing you sought my advice—the very real possibility that your friend, Moxie Mooney, is lying to you from start to finish."

"She'd have to be a pretty good liar."

"Isn't that what an actor is—a pretty good liar?"

"Come on, Marty."

"Consider it as a very real possibility, Fletch. I'm not sitting in judgment of your friend. Sooner or later someone will, I expect. Consider the possibility that she was in this financial razzle-dazzle with Steve Peterman, and that she murdered him only when she discovered she was being swindled, too. My early judgment would be—if I were making a judgment—that your friend, Moxie Mooney, is either awfully guilty or awfully stupid."

"She's just in trouble."

"And she knew it, right?"

"Why do you say that?"

"Why else would you have asked me to go look at Peterman's books?"

"Moxie-the-murderess is a concept I'm having difficulty wrapping my mind around."

Martin Satterlee said: "I'm pretty sure most people who commit murder have a friend somewhere."

25

"You don't look like you slept well," Moxie said. She was looking up at him from a hammock on the second storey of The Blue House.

"Up to a point, I did." Fletch had gone back to bed at a quarter to six, but he had not slept. He listened to the quiet house. He got out of bed again at eight-thirty only because he heard the Lopezes come into the house. He also heard the grinding gears and squeaking brakes of trucks and buses.

In the hammock, Moxie stretched and yawned.

"Thought we'd go sailing today," Fletch said. "We can rent a catamaran on one of the beaches."

"That would be nice."

Somewhere in the house, a window smashed. In

the street in front of the house, someone was yelling.

"Stay here," Fletch said.

On the balcony, he walked around the corner to the front of the house. Gerry and Stella Littleford were already there. They were looking out onto the street. As Fletch approached, they looked at him. On their faces were shock, confusion, anger, hurt, amazement. They said nothing.

In the street in front of The Blue House were two old, rickety yellow school buses, three trucks big enough to carry cattle, a few vans, and some old cars. On the sides of the yellow schoolbuses in big black letters was written SAVE AMERICA.

People from these vehicles were milling in the street. And some of these people wore white hooded robes with eye and nose holes cut in their faces. And others wore brown shirts and brown riding britches and black jackboots and black neckties and black arm bands with red swastikas on them. And some of these people were women in cheap house dresses. And some were children.

"Look at the children," Stella said.

Some men were passing demonstration signs down from the trucks. The signs were passed along from hand to hand. The signs said KEEP AMERICA WHITE, HOLLYWOOD SELLS U.S. SOUL, NO RACIAL MIX. One sign, carefully handprinted, read NO MONGURILIZATION! And these signs came to be held by the men in white hooded robes, and by the women, and by the children.

"I guess they mean me," Gerry Littleford said.

"No," Stella Littleford said. "They mean me."

To the left, the thirty Neo-Nazis were trying to appear military. A man with a red band around his hat was yelling at them as they were lining up. They all had beer bellies they were sucking in while tucking their chins in to show they all had dewlaps.

Moxie was standing beside Fletch and she put her hand on his on the railing.

"These people must have driven all night," Fletch said.

"These aren't people," Moxie said.

In the street someone said, *There's Moxie Mooney,* and *Cunt!, Whore!* were shouted in both men's and women's voices and a voice said, *Isn't that ol' Gerry Littleford up there?* and a rock bounced off the wall of the house behind where they were standing and fell to the floor near their feet.

From one of the trucks, *My country 'tis of thee* began to blare.

Fletch said to Moxie, "You don't think people care about such things anymore? You think there came a moment in history when everyone wised up and love and understanding pervaded the world? Well, it hasn't happened yet, babe. Maybe on television, but not in real life."

Moxie said, "The sick, the stupid, and the scared."

With two rows of uniformed plodgies standing behind him, the man distinguished by a red band around his hat began to shout a speech over the sound of music: *"We all know what this is about! We all know what is happening! We all know what is happening to the world! Who runs Hollywood which makes the movies? The Jews! Who runs the newspapers*

196

which sell the movies? The Jews! Who owns the movie theaters which show the movies? The Jews! Who owns the television networks which push the movies into our homes, spoiling the minds of our children? The Jews! And who pays the Jews? The Communists! The Jewish people do not mix. Oh, no—they do not marry outside their race! They marry outside their race and their families say they're dead! The Russians do not marry outside their race! Oh, no—they send the Jews out of their country...

Moxie giggled. "This is getting confusing."

Along Duval Street, from the houses, guest houses, and coffee shops, and from the side streets ordinary citizens began to appear. They stood apart from these others, their eyes wide, their mouths open. They spoke to each other in disbelief. A large number of them were gathering. A woman shrieked: *Be Nice!* The fishermen began to appear in the crowd, the real fishermen and the sport fishermen and even the other kind of fishermen who always came back to Key West with a full cargo of shrimp they had bought with their other, more valuable cargo. Fletch recognized two or three people who had been at Durty Harry's the night before, listening to Frederick Mooney.

A Cuban-American boy, a Conch, about eight or ten years old, sat cross-legged on the ground behind a man in a white robe. Fletch watched the boy take a cigarette lighter from the pocket of his shorts. It took him five or six tries to get flame from the lighter. Then he set fire to the hem of the man's robe.

...land of liberty...

The man jumped, beat his burning robe with

his arm, and kicked the kid, hard, rolling him over in the gutter. He kicked the kid again, in the head. By then, the robe was burning well. A woman was trying to grab the robe off him. He kept kicking the kid.

The crowd rushed the people who had driven all night. Rocks went through the air in all directions. Sticks appeared from nowhere. Here and there, on bare skin and on the white robes red blood began to appear. Women were screaming, in Cuban and English. The man distinguished by the red band around his hat ordered his uniformed plodgies to drive a wedge through all these screaming, hitting, kicking, yelling people and the uniformed plodgies went into the fray. They were beaten nicely.

From the center of Key West finally there came the sounds of sirens.

Fletch took Moxie's elbow. "Let's go."

"Where we going?"

"Sailing," Fletch said. "It's a nice day for sailing."

Edith Howell in her dressing gown was carrying a cup of coffee up the main stairs of The Blue House. "Something I've never understood," she said to Moxie and Fletch, "is how one can be a Jew and a Communist at the same time. A tree and a stone cannot be the same thing. Either one is one thing, or one is another..."

"Sick people," Moxie answered.

Lopez was waiting in the front hall. He wore a clean white jacket. He said, "Mister Fletcher, Mister Sills is on the phone. He says if I don't put you on the phone, he fires me."

Sy Koller came out of the dining room with his cup of coffee. He said to Moxie, "We're a part of an international conspiracy?"

"Throw 'em a script, Sy," Moxie answered. "Let 'em see how bad it is."

Koller said, "I'd suspect Peterman's hand behind this foolishness—you know, for publicity—if he weren't dead."

Fletch said to Lopez, "Did you tell Sills what's going on outside?"

Outside were the sounds of sirens and hysterical screaming.

"No," said Lopez.

Fletch went down the corridor and through the billiard room to the study.

He lifted the telephone receiver from the desk.

"Good morning, Ted," Fletch said into the phone. "Nice day. We're just going sailing."

"Why am I hearing sirens?"

"Sirens?"

Ted Sills said, "I'm hearing sirens over the phone. While I've been waiting. Was someone singing *My country 'tis of thee . . . ?*"

"I wasn't. Not this morning."

"I heard people screaming. I'm still hearing people screaming."

"Must be a bad connection."

"What's going on there, Fletch?"

"Just settling down for breakfast. Maybe you heard Edith Howell practicing on the scales."

Somewhere in the house another pane of glass smashed.

"What was that?" Ted Sills asked over the phone.

"What was what?"

"Sharp noise. Sounded like glass breaking."

"Must have been at your end, Ted."

"Sounds like a riot's going on."

"Must be your telephone cord, Ted. Give it a tug and see if it clears up."

"Fletcher, I have told you and your little playmates to get out of that house."

"Yes, you did, Ted."

"You're still there."

"Having a few days of peace and quiet."

"I heard on the morning news you're still there. In The Blue House."

"That reminds me, Ted. When does the rubbish get picked up? Want to make sure Lopez puts it out."

"I want you to get out of the goddamned house!" Ted Sills shouted.

"Now, now, Ted. No wonder your phone is broken."

"All right, Fletcher, I'm coming down there. With a shotgun. And if you're not out of that house by the time I get there—"

"You'll hardly be noticed. By the way, Ted, you never told me Moxie Mooney is half-owner of Five Aces Farm."

There was silence from Ted Sill's end of the line. From Fletch's there were three sounds which could have been light-caliber gunshots.

"I happened to find out just this morning," Fletch said. "I didn't know you two knew each other."

Ted Sills said, "Ms Mooney has a financial interest in this farm. What's that to you?"

"Nothing. Just think it odd that here ,you have two such nice financial partners, Moxie and me, staying in your resort house, and you want us out."

"Fletcher..." Ted Sills sighed. "You don't know what you're doing. You've turned that house into a circus."

"Not me, Ted."

Moxie appeared in the doorway of the study. Her eyes were huge. "Stella Littleford's been hurt," she said.

"Sorry, Ted," Fletch said into the phone. "Gotta go."

"What did I just hear?" Sills shouted. "Who's been hurt?"

"The three-minute eggs," said Fletch. "Their feelings are hurt. I'm not there eating 'em."

He hung up and followed Moxie into the front of the house.

Stella Littleford was sitting like a dropped doll on the floor of the front hall. Her hands were over her forehead. Blood was seaping through her fingers.

Sy Koller was kneeling beside her. "Definite need for stiches," he said to Fletch.

The front door was open.

A low haze of riot gas drifted over the street. Police had set up saw horse barricades in a U in the street at the front of The Blue House. Two were knocked over. There were a few discarded white robes on the road. There was also one of the uniformed plodgies sitting on the road in a position nearly identical to Stella Littleford's, another dropped doll, also holding his head.

To the right, down Duval Street, away from the riot gas, hand-to-hand fighting and mouth-to-mouth shouting was continuing.

Directly across the street, a sinewy armed fisherman was puncturing the tires of the school buses and trucks with his fishing knife.

Gerry Littleford ran into the yard followed by two young men with a stretcher. His eyes were red and runny from the gas.

"Shit forever," he said to Fletch. He pointed to a broken rum bottle on the front porch. "Someone pegged Stella with that. Cut her head."

Clearly there had still been rum in the bottle when it broke. The shattered glass was in a puddle.

An ambulance was backing down the street, over one of the fallen saw horses, to the front door of The Blue House.

In the front hall, Mrs Lopez was handing wet cloths to Moxie who was handing them to Sy Koller who was applying them to Stella Littleford's forehead. The young men who brought the stretcher stopped all that. They put a pile of dry gauze against the cut and taped it lightly.

They helped Stella onto the stretcher.

"Want me to go to the hospital with you?" Fletch asked Gerry.

"I do not."

"Want Sy to go?"

Gerry said, "I do not."

"Okay," Fletch said. "I'll see you later."

Gerry followed the stretcher-bearers through the front door.

Fletch stood on the front porch watching them put Stella into the back of the ambulance.

When Moxie joined him, he said. "Watch your feet. Broken glass."

The riot gas was dissipating. A swinging, kicking crowd came back down Duval Street from the right, knocking over another barricade. Fletch supposed the demonstrators were trying to get back to their buses and trucks. Their signs were broken and trampled around the trucks as were record player and the amplifiers. The trucks, the buses, and some of the cars had flat tires. But by then there were too many personal angers and personal scores to settle and the pushing and the punching continued.

From above their heads, from the upper front balcony of The Blue House boomed the world's best trained, most voluminous voice: *"Four score and seven years ago..."*

"Oh, God," said Moxie.

In fact, the people in the street did look up. That's Frederick Mooney! And they did stop fighting.

"...our forefathers brought forth on this continent..."

"Good ol' Freddy," said Fletch. "Let's go sailing."

"...a new nation..."

Fletch and Moxie walked through the house to the back. Even in the backyard they could hear

Mooney's *Gettysburg Address.* All other noises had ceased.

"Think of that volume of sound," Moxie said, "coming out of a head that must hurt as much as his does!"

26

After they sailed awhile, Moxie said, "I suppose I should ask you, seeing it wasn't so long ago you put me on an airplane ostensibly for dinner and landed me far enough away from the scene of the crime to make me a fugitive from justice, if now you have me in a sailboat, do you mean to flee the country with me?"

"Damn," said Fletch at the tiller. "You caught me. You penetrated my purposeful plot."

Moxie's eyes were full of the sunlight reflected from the sea. "I've always heard Cuba is a gorgeous country."

Up to that point, they had said little to each other.

They had walked to a Cuban-American restaurant and had a quiet breakfast. Some of the people there had recognized Moxie and smiled at her in a friendly way and kept their dignity by otherwise leaving her alone. During breakfast, Moxie wondered aloud if Stella Littleford would have a scar on her forehead forever and Fletch said he thought Stella had suffered a concussion as well because there had been quite a lot of rum in the bottle that had hit her. The *senora* of that restaurant made a picnic lunch for them and put it in a cardboard box. Fletch also bought a six-pack of cold soft drinks.

They walked the long way around, along the water, until they came to a beach where Fletch rented a catamaran. He put the food and the drinks aboard. Boys on the beach helped them push the catamaran into the surf. Fletch boosted Moxie aboard and then climbed aboard himself.

The process of launching put enough water in the bottom of the boat to soak the cardboard picnic box. Moxie showed Fletch the soggy box as he was finding the wind and beginning to sail on it and they laughed. She rescued the sandwiches and the fruit and rolled the box into a ball and dropped it into the bottom of the boat.

Moxie was wearing her bikini and she removed the top but she kept herself more or less in the shade of the sail. She said, "Talk to me."

"About what?"

"Something nice, please."

"Edith Howell says if you're not talking you're dead, or something."

"If Edith Howell ever stopped talking everyone else would die. Of shock."

"She has her eyes on your father's millions."

Moxie snorted. "Millions of empty cognac bottles. She's welcome to 'em." She put herself on her side and trailed her fingers in the water. "Talk to me about something nice. Like how come you're so rich."

"You're asking me if I'm rich?"

"Well, you're not working. You have that nice place in Italy."

"That's sort of a rude question, from a girl I just met."

"I know. Answer me anyway."

"It's a long story."

"I've got all day."

"It's sort of an impossible story to tell. In detail."

"Did you do something wrong, Fletch? Are you a crook?"

"Who, me? No. I don't think so."

"What happened?"

"Not much. One night I found myself alone in a room with a lot of cash. The cash was there because I had been hired to do a bad thing. I had not done the bad thing. But the bad thing had happened anyway. Coincidentally."

"Boy, why don't you spare me a few details?"

"I told you it's a long story."

"So you took the money..."

"I had to. Leaving it there would have embarrassed people. It would have raised questions."

"Robbery as an act of kindness?"

"I thought so at the time."

"What did you do with the money?"

"I didn't know what to do with it. I had never been very good with money."

"No foolin'. I remember the time..."

"What time?"

"Forget it. I'm still mad."

"There should never be money between friends."

"That's it," said Moxie. "There wasn't any. Unfortunately, you had invited me to one of Los Angeles' most posh eateries."

"Oh. That time."

"That time."

"Yes."

"I wouldn't mind getting my watch back sometime. The one the restaurant took."

"A Piaget, wasn't it?"

"With little diamonds."

Fletch asked, "What time is it?"

She put herself on her stomach. "Who cares?"

Fletch said: "Exactly."

Moxie inhaled slowly and exhaled with a great sigh. "Oh, Fletch. Oh, Fletch—you never change."

He smiled at her, showing her all his front teeth. "I just get better."

"Worse. So what did you do with all this money you stole?"

"I didn't steal it."

"It just fell into your lap."

"Something like that. Long story. The money was on its way to South America, see, so I went with it. I'm very big on seeing actions completed. Essential to my psyche."

"Then how come you haven't finished writing the biography of Edgar Arthur Tharp?"

"I'm working on it. I was in South America. I didn't know what to do with the money. Maybe I felt a little badly about having it. Maybe I was trying to get rid of it. So I bought gold with it."

"Oh, no."

"I did."

"And the price of gold shot up?"

"Someone mentioned that to me. In a bar. So I felt worse. I got rid of the gold. Quick. Yuck. I hated the oil companies, thought they were given' the world a royal screwin', they were bound to get their comeuppance—"

"So you put your money into oil companies?"

"Yes. I did."

"And their value shot up?"

"So I heard. That made me feel worse."

"I can believe."

"I got rid of that yucky stuff as quick as I could. I've done terribly."

"And where's the money now?"

"Well, I decided my investment policy wasn't very sound. Very responsible. You know what I mean? I had been buying things I didn't like."

"So you decided to buy things you did like?"

"I decided to use the money to help out, instead of hinder. I heard General Motors was having such a tough time nobody was buying its stock."

"So you bought General Motors?"

"So I bought General Motors. And the cable-electronic companies looked risky, so I put some money into them."

"Good Lord, Fletch. God! You're so incompetent!"

"Well, I never said I was any good with money."

"You should have taken a course. *How To Invest.*"

"Yes," Fletch said. "I suppose I should have."

"You just never cared about money!"

"No," said Fletch. "I don't."

When they got to the Gulf Stream she went overboard and he lowered the sails and, except for the light lines to the boat he tied to his ankles, he got naked, too, and went overboard and they played and made love in the water, only the light, drifting boat kept pulling him away from her by the ankles and he kept getting too much water up his nose and they both laughed so hard they ran out of breath and nearly drowned but they did succeed, but they were slow to leave the water and climb back into the boat anyway.

"As long as we're talking about money," he said.

"Is this still nice talk?"

"Jumping Cow Productions, Incorporated," he said.

They had sailed back to an empty beach and run the catamaran up onto the fine sand. They took their food and drinks ashore and had a picnic. The drinks were very warm but they drank them anyway, for the sake of putting fluid into their bodies. The sandwiches had dried out. Mostly they ate the fruit.

After eating, they lay in the sand. It was late enough in the afternoon and there were enough passing clouds so the sun would not burn their tanned skin. Fletch waited a long while. Finally she put herself on her side and she put her hand on his hip and he put himself on his side as well and put his head on his hand. Her face told him he had her attention, but she did not expect to talk about money at this time.

"Tell me, Moxie," he said. "What does the cow jump over?"

"The moon," she answered easily. Then her face changed. She looked at him as if he had struck her. Then she rolled over onto her back. She covered her eyes with one hand. "Mooney," she groaned.

"Right. Moxie Mooney." She continued to lay flat on her back beside him on the sand, her hand covering her eyes from the sun. "You are sole proprietor of Jumping Cow Productions, Incorporated. Martin Satterlee called me this morning."

"Good." She rolled onto her stomach. "I'll close that Goddamned movie down faster than anything you ever saw."

"Midsummer Night's Madness?"

"Fini to *Midsummer Night's Madness.* To Edith Howell, Sy Koller, Geoff McKensie, Gerry Littleford, Talcott Cross, the whole damned bunch of 'em. Goodbye to that stupid script. Goodbye to Route 41."

"I take it you did not know you are sole proprietor of Jumping Cow Productions?"

"I did not. I certainly did not."

"Moxie, when you went into Peterman's office— a couple of weeks ago—what did you actually learn? What did you actually find out that upset you so, you know, enough to cause you to ask me to meet you here?"

"I couldn't find any real tax reports. I kept

asking the staff for the tax files. They kept bringing me folder after folder with all this crazy stuff in them, loan agreements with banks in Honduras and Switzerland and Mexico. I didn't know what it all meant, but I got madder and madder." Her voice dropped. "Or more and more scared."

Fletch lay back on the sand, folding his hands behind his head. "Marty couldn't do a very thorough job of looking at your financial records. Four o'clock this morning the police came in and took them all."

"Oh, God! The police have my financial records?"

"You knew they—"

"I didn't know anything, Fletch!" Moxie snapped. She pounded her fist on the sand. "Damn!"

She got up and walked at an angle down the beach to the water's edge and then kept walking along the water.

After a long while, when she didn't come back he took their garbage back to the boat and turned it around in the light surf and otherwise prepared for departure.

Then he sat on one of the hulls and waited while Moxie walked back down the beach.

They launched the boat together.

"Moxie?" Again they were sailing, the low sun at their stern. She sat, the picture of dejection, chin on hand, elbow on knee. "You know the guy who owns The Blue House?"

"No. How could I?"

"His name is Ted Sills. You said yesterday you don't know him."

"I don't."

"Apparently you are a co-owner with Ted Sills of a Florida horse farm."

She wrinkled her face at him. There was salt on her skin and a small dab of sand on one cheekbone. "We're partners in something?"

"Five Aces Farm. Ocala, Florida."

She shrugged. "News to me."

"I guess he was a friend of Steve Peterman's."

"Listen, Fletch." She sounded tired and angry and tired of being angry. "Why don't you just give it to me in simple?"

"Wish I could. As I told you, Marty didn't get very far into your records when the cops arrived. He seems to agree with your two main fears: that you are in tax trouble; that you do owe huge and unlikely sums of money to banks all over the world."

Moxie Mooney looked all over the horizon. "Which way did you say Cuba is?"

He pointed. "That way."

"You want to come with me, or should I start swimming?"

"An awful lot of inexplicable financial activity has been going on under your name."

"Inexplicable . . . and you expect me to explain?"

"Marty couldn't explain it. He couldn't understand it."

"Is it your friend Marty's opinion that something crooked has been going on?"

"He was trying not to have an opinion."

"But he had to try hard, right?"

"Right." Fletch hitched in the main sheet. "He

213

seemed to feel all that much activity couldn't have been going on without your knowing about it."

The red light from the setting sun full in her face, Moxie just stared at Fletch.

Fletch said, quietly: "In other words, Moxie, chances are pretty good your average judge is going to believe you're lying."

"Lying," she said.

"About everything."

She looked at the paper sandwich wrappers and empty soda cans on the deck of the cockpit. "The way you were lying this morning? About all your money?"

Fletch chuckled. "Yeah."

"Come on, Fletch. Games are games. This isn't fun."

She studied the junk in the bottom of the boat a long time.

Then she put her hand on his knee. "Hey, Fletch. Thanks for the nice day."

"Nice to make your acquaintance," he said.

He was sailing for the right beach. Leaving that morning he had lined the beach up with the martello towers.

"In other words," Moxie said, "going through my financial records, the cops are going to find I had tons of reasons for killing Steve Peterman."

"It looks that way."

The centerboard was up. Near the beach, Fletch was looking for the heads of late swimmers on the water.

"Fletch." Moxie shivered. "Please find someone else to pin this murder on."

"I'm tryin', babe," Fletch said. "I'm tryin'."

It was dark and walking through the side streets in her loose beach wrap, her head down, Moxie attracted no attention.

Fletch said, "There's one other small matter..."

"Boy, you're really giving it to me today. I thought we were just going to talk about happy things."

"I got you out of the house just so we could talk."

"You took me sailing so you could beat up on me."

"Your father told me about your going to school in England..."

Quietly, Moxie said, "You knew I went to school in England. Almost two years."

"I never knew why."

"Freddy was being paternal that year. Wanted me near him."

"But he wasn't in England that year."

"He was supposed to be. His schedule got changed."

"Moxie..." Fletch took her hand. "Hey," he said. "Your father said something about your drama coach at school getting murdered."

Her hand went limp in his. "I was only fourteen."

"God! What does that mean?"

She pulled her hand from his. "It means Freddy didn't think I needed all that pressure on me at the age of fourteen!"

"'Pressure'! 'Pressure'?"

She veered on the rough sidewalk. They were then on a dark, empty sidestreet. She was walking a meter away from him. "Do you think I murdered Mister Hodes?"

"'Think', I don't think anything. I didn't even know the guy's name."

"He was a little shit," Moxie muttered.

"I think you were gotten out of town damned fast. Way out. Out of the country. And you went."

"I was fourteen, for God's sake." They had stopped walking. "I didn't mind going to school in England. It sounded cool."

"I ask you if you murdered somebody and all you say is you were fourteen!"

"Is that what you think? You think I murdered the birdy drama coach?"

"I don't know what to think. I hate what I think. Why don't you answer me?"

Across the sidewalk her eyes glowered.

"Think what you want, Fletcher."

She began to walk. She walked with her fists clenched at her sides.

She walked ahead of him all the way to the house.

They approached The Blue House from the rear.

Moxie, well ahead of him, head down, zipped through the back gate into the garden.

When Fletch got to the back gate Lopez was coming through with a rubbish barrel.

"Ah," Fletch said. "Tomorrow's the day the rubbish gets picked up."

Lopez grinned at him. "A lot of broken glass, Mister Fletcher. They threw a lot of stones."

"I know. Any real damage?"

"No. It's all cleaned up. Tomorrow I will start replacing the windows which were broken."

On top of the barrel that Lopez had just set down were three empty apple juice bottles.

"Sorry about this morning," Fletch said. "All the noise. Damage. Mess. Guess I'm not a very good tenant."

Lopez' grin grew even broader. "It's fun," he said. "This house is empty so much. The excitement is good. Don't think about it."

27

"How many stitches?" Fletch asked.

In the hospital bed Stella Littleford didn't look any more sallow than usual. The surgical dressing on her forehead was not as big as Fletch expected.

"Six." She did not smile.

Gerry Littleford sat in a side chair, his feet propped up on the bed. On top of his shorts he was wearing a hospital johnny. He had left The Blue House that morning without a shirt. Apparently he had not been back to the house since. He also wore paper slippers on his feet.

"They're keeping her overnight," Gerry said. "Concussion."

"I brought you some flowers," Fletch said. "Nurse ate them." He crossed the room and leaned his back against the window sill. "What happened this morning anyway? I didn't see...I was on the phone."

"There was a riot," Gerry Littleford said drily.

"I went out into the front yard and shook my fists at those dirty bastards and called them dirty bastards," Stella said. "Dirty bastards."

"Does it hurt to talk?"

"It does now." She tried not to laugh. "It didn't this morning."

"She got bonked," Gerry said. "Someone threw a rum bottle at her."

"Someone must have really cared," Fletch said. "There was still rum in the bottle."

"Good." Stella again tried not to laugh.

"I've never seen you laugh before," Fletch said to her.

"She does everything she's not supposed to do," Gerry said, "when she's not supposed to do it. Like marrying me."

Stella's eyes moved slowly to Gerry's face. Fletch could not read the expression in them.

"Question," Fletch said. "Have either of you heard before from these groups? Threatening letters, phone calls, anything?"

Neither answered him.

"I'm just wondering," Fletch said, "how much these groups wanted that film stopped."

Still, neither answered him.

"Hey," Fletch said. "There's been a murder. Maybe two. Stella's in bed with a concussion. Stitches in her forehead. This morning we saw demonstrations demanding the film be stopped. It's a reasonable question."

Gerry asked, "Has the film been stopped?"

And Fletch didn't answer. "Have you heard from any of these groups before?"

Gerry put his feet flat on the floor and sat straight in his chair as if about to give testimony in court. "To be honest—yes."

"Letters?"

"With pamphlets enclosed. Keep-the-white-race-pure pamphlets. You know? So you honkies can go a few more centuries without soul."

"There have been phone calls, too, Gerry," Stella said.

"Phone calls," Gerry said.

"Threats?"

"My black ass will get burned, if I make the film. I'll get a shot in the head." Gerry's eyes roamed over Fletch's face. "It's hard for a black man to tell a real threat from normal white man's conversation."

"Did you tell anybody about these threats?"

"Like who?"

"Anybody in authority. Steve Peterman. Talcott what's-his-name. Sy Koller. The cops."

"You think I'm crazy? Making this film is my employment. I'm not lookin' to get unemployed."

"Do you still have any of these letters, pamphlets?"

"'Course not. Throw 'em away. Gotta throw 'em away."

"Do you remember any of the names, groups that sent you these letters?"

"They all have these long, phony names. You know: My Land But Not Your Land Committee Incorporated; Society To Keep 'em Pickin' Cotton."

"You got a call from a black group, too, Gerry."

"Yes, I did." Gerry smiled. "Some of the brothers want to keep soul to ourselves a few more centuries."

"Gerry," Fletch asked, "sincerely—do you think the production of *Midsummer Night's Madness* seriously was being threatened by any of these groups? Like to the point of murder?"

"I don't know. They're madmen. How can you tell when madmen are serious?" More quietly, he said, "Yeah. I think there were murderers in that group this morning that attacked the house. People capable of murder. Plenty of 'em. That rum bottle coulda killed Stella. I just doubt they're up to organizing anything as clever as the murder of Steve Peterman. Whoever got Steve was no dope."

"I guess you're right."

The nurse brought in a vase of roses. There were no other flowers in the room.

"Ah!" Fletch got off the window sill. "You didn't eat 'em."

"I had supper at home," the nurse said. "Daffodils."

Fletch was at the door. "Coming back to the house, Gerry?"

"Sure," he said. "Later."

28

In the cool night, Fletch walked around Key West for awhile. He found himself in the center of the old commercial district so he went down the alley to Durty Harry's. Frederick Mooney was not there. Few were. There was no band playing either.

He sat at the bar and ordered a beer. A clock he had seen said ten minutes past eleven but clocks in Key West are not expected to tell the real time. Clocks in Key West are only meant to substantiate unreality.

A dog, a black dog, a large black dog walked through the bar at the heels of a man who came through a door on the second storey and down a spiral staircase.

"What's that dog's name?" Fletch asked the young woman behind the bar.

"That's Emperor. Isn't he a nice dog?"

"Nice dog." Fletch sipped his beer. He did not want the beer. The early morning phone call from Satterlee, the demonstrations, the day of sailing and swimming in the wind and sun made him glad to sit quietly a moment. He thought about Global Cable News and how quickly his phone call had been answered and he was allowed to speak to that hour's producer because he was a stockholder. It should be the story that counts, not who is calling it in. Anything can be checked out. Your average stockholder is not any more honest or accurate than your average citizen. Fletch decided if he ever had a big story again he'd call it into Global Cable News under a phony name. It would be an interesting experiment—for a stockholder. He wanted to sleep. He left the rest of his beer on the bar. "Nice dog," he said.

29

Something woke him up. It was dawn. Fletch remained in bed a minute listening to the purposeful quiet. It was too purposeful.

He got out of bed and went out onto the balcony.

There were two policemen in the sideyard. They looked back up at him.

In the dawn he could see the flashing blue lights of police cars at the front of the house.

"Shit," Fletch said.

He ran along the balcony against the wall to the back of the house and around the corner. Gerry Littleford was curled up asleep in a hammock.

Fletch shook his shoulder. "Gerry. Wake up. It may be a bust."

Gerry opened one eye to him. "What? A what?"

Were the police there to arrest someone for murder? No, there were too many of them. There were now three cops in the backyard. Were they there because they had been tipped off there would be another demonstration? No, they were in the yard. Some judge had given them a warrant to be on and in the property.

"It sure looks like a bust to me," Fletch said quietly.

"A bust?"

"Shut up. Get up. Get rid of whatever shit you have." Fletch pulled up on one side of the hammock and Gerry fell out the other side landing like a panther on braced fingers and toes. "Down the toilet, Gerry. *Pronto.*"

In the bedroom Fletch put on his shorts and shirt.

"What's happening?" Moxie said into her pillow.

"You might get dressed. The cops are here."

Instantly she sat up. Instantly there was no sign of sleep in her face. Instead there was the look of someone cornered, frightened but who would fight.

"I know," Fletch said. "You didn't kill Steve Peterman. Ho-hum."

And three policemen were standing on the front porch. When Fletch opened the front door to them they seemed surprised. They had not rung the bell or knocked.

"Good morning," Fletch said. "Welcome to the home of the stars. Donations are tax deductible."

The policemen seemed shy. There were five police cars in the street. The roof lights of three were flashing. Despite the demonstration the day before, the street was clean.

Fletch held his hand out to them, palm up. A policeman put a folded paper into Fletch's palm. Nevertheless, he said, "May we come in?"

Fletch held their own paper up to them. "Guess this says you may."

In the front hall one of the policemen said, "I'm Sergeant Henning."

Fletch shook hands with him. "Fletcher. Tenant of this domicile."

"We have to search this domicile."

"Sure," Fletch said. "Coffee?"

The sergeant looked around at all the other policemen coming into the house, through the front and back and verandah doors, and said, "Sure."

In the kitchen Fletch put a pan of water on the stove and got out two mugs. "Thanks for your help yesterday."

"Actual fact, we weren't much help. Got here late. Things had gone too far. Things like that don't happen here in Key West anyway."

"Not on your daily agenda, huh?"

"Actual fact, sort of hard to know what to do. Those bimbos are citizens, too. Sort of got the right to demonstrate."

"Were there any actual arrests?" Fletch spooned instant coffee into the two mugs. From upstairs he could hear people moving around. Furniture being moved. Then he could hear Edith Howell's voice pitched high in indignation.

"Nine. They'll be released this morning."

"No one threw that rum bottle at Mrs. Littleford, huh?" The water in the pan was bubbling.

"None of the people we arrested did." The sergeant smiled ruefully. "We asked every one of 'em, we did. Politely, too."

Fletch poured the water into the mugs and handed one to the police sergeant.

"Any sugar?" the sergeant asked. Fletch nodded to the bowl on the counter. "I need my sugar." The sergeant helped himself. "Coffee and sugar. It's what keeps me bad-tempered."

Two other policemen came into the kitchen and began searching through it.

"Appreciate it if you wouldn't make too much of a mess," Fletch said. "Know Mrs. Lopez?"

"Sure," a cop said.

"She'll have to clean up."

He went out onto the back porch with his coffee. The sergeant followed him.

"Can you tell me why you're searching the house?" Fletch asked.

The sergeant shrugged. "Illegal substances."

"Yeah, but why? What's the evidence you had to get a warrant?"

"It was good enough for the judge. That sure is a nice banyan tree. I haven't been in this house in years." He grinned at Fletch. "You in the movies, too?"

"No."

"Just one of those cats who likes to associate with movie people, huh?"

"Yeah. A hanger-on."

"It must be sort of disappointin', seein' these

227

people up close. I mean, when no one's writin' their lines for 'em, no one's directin' how they act. I'd rather leave 'em on the screen."

"I'm sure they'd rather be left on the screen."

"That Mister Mooney sure is one big drunk. Seen him downtown. He needs a keeper."

"He's a great man."

"One of our patrolmen drove him home the other night. First night you were here."

"Thank you."

"Chuck said Mooney recited all the way home." The sergeant chuckled. "Something about Jessie James being due in town. Better watch out for him." The sergeant drank some coffee. Upstairs Edith Howell was exclaiming, proclaiming, declaiming. "This whole country's drunk. Stoned on something."

"Whole world."

"The people have discovered drugs. Not enough to do any more. Machines do the hard work. Recreational drugs, we're callin' 'em now. Baseball is recreation ... fishin'. Too much time."

"Not everyone can go fishin'. Not everyone can go to baseball."

"The whole damned world's stoned on one thing or another."

Saying nothing, a policeman held the back door open. His eyes were bloodshot.

The sergeant left his coffee mug on the kitchen counter. The kitchen was really very clean.

John Meade was standing in the front hall. A policeman was standing beside him. John Meade was wearing gray slacks and brown loafers and a blue button-down shirt and handcuffs.

He smiled at Fletch. "Ludes."

"Sorry, John," said Fletch. "I never thought of you."

"Brought 'em back from New York."

The sergeant took a tin container from the policeman. "Qualudes," the sergeant said. "A controlled substance. You have a prescription, Mister Meade?"

"My doctor died," John Meade said. "Eleven years ago."

"Sorry to hear that. I sure liked you in *Easy River*."

"So did I," said John Meade.

The sergeant was examining the tin box. "You sure didn't get this from any legitimate source, Mister Meade. You're supportin' the bad guys, actual fact."

Other police were coming into the front hall.

"Hey, Sergeant," Fletch said. "Does this have to happen? Do you have to take Mister Meade in?"

"Yeah," Sergeant Hennings said. "Too many witnesses. Too many cops around."

30

Fletch retreated to the small study at the back of The Blue House.

On the front stairs Edith Howell was screaming her rage that the police had taken John Meade away in handcuffs. She was screaming at Frederick Mooney to go do something about it. There had not been a sound from Frederick Mooney. Fletch wasn't even sure he was in the house. Edith Howell was dressed in blue silk pajamas, blue silk slippers, and a blue silk robe. Her hair was in pin curls and her face clotted with cream. Sy Koller's head had appeared over the second-floor bannister looking painfully hung-over. Lopez and Gerry Littleford were in the backyard throwing a tennis ball back and forth. Mrs. Lopez was in the kitchen making real coffee, starting breakfast. Neither Geoffrey McKensie nor Moxie had come down.

Fletch did not mind telephoning Five Aces Farm that early in the morning. Horse people are always up early.

The phone rang so long without being answered Fletch sat at the desk.

Finally a man's voice answered.

"This is Fletcher. May I speak with Mister Sills, please?"

"Not here, Mister Fletcher. This is Max Frizzlewhit."

"Mornin', Max. Ted must have been off pretty early. Is there a race somewhere?"

"Yeah, there's a race. But he's not at it. I'm just about to go with the trailer. 'Cept the phone kept ringin' and ringin' down here at the stables. One of your horses, too, Mister Fletcher," Frizzlewhit sped along in his English accent. "Scarlet Pimple-Nickle. Call to wish her luck?"

"Does she have a chance?"

"No. If she had half a chance we would have moved her to the track yesterday. She's not worth stable fees."

"Then why are you running her?"

"She needs the exercise."

"Oh, good."

"She needs the experience."

"Will she ever be any good, Max?"

"No."

"Then why do I own her?"

"Beats me. She may have looked good that week you were here."

"Never again?"

"And never before, I think."

"Maybe I brought something out in her."

"Maybe. You ought to come by more often, Mister Fletcher."

"To buy more horses?"

"You ought to go to the track."

"It's too embarrassing, Max."

"Maybe if you went to the track ol' Scarlet Pimple-Nickle would perform for you, keep her eye on the finish instead of on a bunch of horses' asses." If only the horses he trained ran as fast as Frizzlewhit talked...

"This horse has an anal fixation, is that it?"

"I'm not sure she's an actual pervert, Mister Fletcher. It just may be that she'd never seen anything but other horses' asses."

"Very understanding of you, Frizzlewhit."

"Hey, you have to be, in this business. Horses are just like people."

"No," Fletch said. "They're smarter. They don't invest in people and make 'em run around a track."

"That's true. They are smarter that way."

"So where did Mister Sills go?"

"He left the country."

"Ah. Was this a sudden trip, would you say?"

"He packed and left last night. He was plannin' to go to the race today."

"A sudden trip. Did he mention which country he's favoring?"

"France. He mentioned France."

"And which way was he going?"

"By airplane, Mister Fletcher."

"I mean, through Miami? New York?"

"Atlanta, I think."

"Then he's gone. Left the country."

"Can't be sure. Cousin Heath, from Piddle—you know I had a cousin lives in Piddle?—came to see me and got into that Atlanta airport and wasn't heard from Tuesday noon till Saturday teatime. Said he kept expectin' somethin' to happen, and nothin' did."

"I'm going to tell people to keep their eye on you, Frizzlewhit."

"Wish you would. Sometimes it gets lonely down here with the horses."

"Even you can outrun 'em, huh?"

"Some of 'em are no improvement over stayin' still."

"Will Mister Sills call you?"

"Prolly."

"You might tell him The Blue House was busted this morning. For drugs."

"Yeah? You had a rave-up down there just yesterday, didn't you? Nasties and the bedsheet bunch. Saw it on television, I did. What's going to happen tomorrow?"

"That's always the question, isn't it?"

"That's what makes a horse race."

"Damn," said Fletch. "I didn't think you knew what makes a horse race."

And Fletch did not mind telephoning Chief of Detectives Roz Nachman at that early hour. Police stations are supposed to be open for twenty-four-hour-a-day service. If she wasn't there yet he should be able to leave a message.

But she was there.

"Aren't you getting any sleep at all, Chief?"

"Thank you for your concern, Mister Fletcher."

"Thank you."

"For what?"

"Staging that drug bust this morning. Here at The Blue House. I'm sure I'll figure out why in a minute. Trying to discover who's sleeping with whom? You could have asked. You did before."

"How's the weather in Key West?"

"Nice."

"It's nice here, too."

"Having John Meade busted in Key West for a few qualudes is not nice of you."

"John Meade?"

"He could end up with a jail sentence, you know. He's a big name. Make good headlines for the authorities in Key West."

"Was he in illegal possession of a controlled substance?"

"That's why he's being held."

"I'm sorry. Loved him in *Easy River*."

"So did he. He won't be able to use his talents to give you much more pleasure if he's in the hoosegow."

"So I'll see *Easy River* again. It's on the T.V. all the time. Now—regarding that question you asked? Regarding Steven Peterman's car?"

"Yes?"

"We had it checked out. The car was in the parking lot on Bonita Beach. A blue Cadillac."

"A rented car?"

"Yes. No damage. Not a scrape. So that's the end of that great line of investigation."

"What date did he rent the car?"

There was a long silence from Chief of Detectives Roz Nachman. "That's a good point. Are you trying to get ahead of me, Mister Fletcher?"

"Would you expect him to keep a damaged car? A damaged rented car?"

"I wonder what date he actually arrived in Florida."

"I don't know. I should think you'd know by now."

"I would, too. Okay ..."

"So that line of investigation is still open?"

"We'll check further."

"Another thing. You must know that yesterday we had sort of a riot here. A demonstration. Some violence."

"It was in all the papers. On T.V. Everybody's name mentioned but your's. Who are you, Mister Fletcher?"

"Chief, one of these groups might really have been trying to stop this film. I mean, to the point of murder. Gerry Littleford said last night that he had received threatening letters and phone calls—"

"Does he have any of the letters?"

"No. But the riot yesterday—Stella Littleford did

235

get hurt. Some of these people can be vicious. Insanely vicious.

"Vicious but not smart. I don't think your average bigoted tub-of-lard is up to getting on location and then making a knife magically appear between the ribs of somebody sitting on a well-lit stage in daylight surrounded by cameras.... Do you, earwig?"

"No."

"Keep trying, earwig. Things are looking worse and worse for your Ms Moxie Mooney. I need a devil's advocate."

"What do you mean?"

"Well, all those film experts we hired—they're coming down pretty heavily on her. That dance she did."

"What dance?"

"Didn't you see her? Thought you were there."

"What dance?"

"Just before the, you know, murder. Moxie Mooney got up from her chair and did a little dance. She was showing Dan Buckley some little dance step she did in *A Broadway Hit.*"

"In her bathrobe?"

"Make-up robe, dressing gown, whatever you want to call it. It's terrycloth. We have it. I should think it would be too big for her."

"So she couldn't have done it."

"So she could have. After she did her little dance step, she went back to her own chair, crossing behind where Peterman and Buckley were sitting."

"She crossed behind them."

236

"Yes. Behind. It's in all the videotapes. In fact, it looks a little unnatural. From where she finished her dance, she could have walked directly back to her chair, or behind Peterman and Buckley. She chose to walk behind them."

"Oh, God."

"The experts have drawn lines all over the stage floor. They talk in cubes. Do you understand that?"

"No."

"Neither do I. Upshot of it is they said it would have been more direct, and more natural for her to walk in front of the men. It looks a little unnatural to me. But, keep tryin', earwig. Believe me, I'd rather find some group of crazies guilty of murder than Moxie Mooney. This is not the way I want to become a famous detective."

"Are there any other leads you're following?"

"Sure. But let me keep a few secrets, will you? Again I warn you, Fletcher: don't you and Ms Mooney leave Key West, except to come back here."

"I hear you."

"Some people were a little nervous when you went sailing yesterday."

"You know about that?"

"The Coast Guard did a helicopter over you."

"Oh, no."

"Oh, yes. They said you were real cute together. Said it was just like watching a movie."

31

"Cats will bark before I ever accept an invitation to stay in your house again, Mister What's-your-name Fletcher," Edith Howell stated at breakfast.

"What Katz?" asked Sy Koller. "Sam Katz or Jock Katz?"

They were crowded at the white iron framed glass table on the cistern in the backyard of The Blue House. Moxie had not yet come down to breakfast.

"A riot out of control one morning. People throwing rocks at the house. Bopping poor Stella with a bottle. Why didn't you call the police?"

"Jock Katz always barked," Sy Koller said. "He barked all the time."

"A police raid this morning, at dawn. They

came right into my bedroom while I was sleeping! I threw my aspirin bottle at the damned cop. Hit him, too, right on the cheek."

"Sam Katz never barked. Sam was a pussy cat."

"And they yank John off and charge him with being in possession of medicine, or something..."

"Are you saying we were raided by the police this morning?" Frederick Mooney asked.

"We were, Freddy." Edith put her hand on his. "Isn't it terrible?"

Mooney extricated his hand to deal with the grapefruit. "Never heard a thing."

"They swarmed all over the house, Freddy," Edith said.

"Like roaches," grinned Gerry Littleford.

"You mean they entered and searched my bedroom while I slept?" Freddy asked.

"Yes, dear," commiserated Edith.

"How forward of them," said Freddy. "I trust I was sleeping well."

"I'm sure you were sleeping handsomely, dear."

Lopez poured orange juice into Fletch's glass. "Global Cable News is on the phone."

"Tell them I'll call them back, please."

"Fletcher," Edith Howell asked, "do you realize one of your houseguests is in the hospital and another is in prison?"

"We're dropping like flies," Koller said through a mouthful of scrambled egg.

"Roaches," said Gerry Littleford.

"You Yanks don't see the comic side of anything," Geoff McKensie said.

Sy Koller stopped chewing and stared at him.

Moxie appeared in her bikini with a light, white open linen top.

"Good morning, sweets," Edith gushed.

Gerry Littleford squeezed against Sy Koller to make room for her.

Fletch hitched his chair sideways. One leg stuck in a crack. Looking down, he jumped the chair leg out of the crack. On top of the cistern was a half-meter cut square. East and west on the square were hinged lift-rings.

"Did you sleep?" Mooney asked his daughter. "I hear there was a disturbance."

Lopez was back with a fresh pot and poured Moxie's coffee.

"Anybody know how these old cisterns work?" asked Fletch.

"Might as well get it over," Moxie said. She sipped her black coffee. "I've heard from the producers." She gave Fletch a long, solemn look, warning him not to correct her. "The production is cancelled."

Thus was almost everybody at breakfast fired. Geoffrey McKensie had already been fired.

Mooney did not permit the silence to last too long. "Is that the production of *Midsummer Night's Dream*, daughter?"

"O.L.!" she said in exasperation.

"That's too bad." Mooney's eyes ran up the banyan tree. "I was rather hoping to be offered a part."

"But why?" Edith had caught her breath. "Everything was going so well." Moxie snorted. "Well, at least I think so, and I'm sure John would back

240

me up, if he weren't in jail for medicine. My part was the best I've had in a long time. I was doing so well at it. With the help of dear Sy, of course."

"Who did you speak to?" Gerry Littleford asked.

"Didn't quite catch the name," Moxie answered. "It was a legitimate phone call."

Sy Koller asked: "Why did they call you?"

"I just happened to answer the phone." Moxie Mooney was lying well. "We're all relieved of our contracts as of today."

"Fired," Gerry Littleford said.

"Ah, the vicissitudes of this business," consoled Mooney.

"But it's not fair!" said Edith. "I sublet my apartment in New York. I gave up a perfectly good legitimate theater offer. Where will I go, what will I do? Freddy!"

"Yes?" Mooney answered formally, stiff-arming being called upon.

"Well, McKensie," Sy Koller looked the man straight in the eyes. "Looks like your suit against Jumping Cow Productions won't be much good to you now."

"Damed fools." McKensie had reddened beneath his tan. "Too cheap to take a few days proper mourning for the director's wife yet when a few congenital idiots wrap themselves in bedsheets and throw a few rocks at a house, they collapse and cancel the production, losing everything they've invested in it!"

"Are such things insured?" Fletch asked.

"You've got to look on the comic side of things,

241

McKensie," Sy Koller said. Koller was not laughing, or smiling, or looking at all pleased.

"It's the bad publicity that killed it," Moxie said. "The man said."

"There's no such thing as bad publicity," said Edith Howell. "Especially these days. Any publicity is good. The more the better. Murder, riots, raids. Why we've been top of the news three days running! And the film isn't even made yet. Freddy, tell them there's no such thing as bad publicity."

"It's not only the bad publicity," Moxie said. "The press has begun to refer to *Midsummer Night's Madness* as a badly-written, cheaply-produced exploitation picture. The film will never live down its reputation now."

"Even if you use my script," McKensie said. "Even if I direct. I don't want anything to do with it."

Koller smiled. "And thus dies a lawsuit. We all heard you say that, McKensie. We're all witnesses."

Gerry Littleford asked, quietly, "Are they saying this picture exploits the race issue?"

Moxie took a deep breath. "Yes. Of course. Somebody must have gotten ahold of a script. Gratuitous violence, in black and white and color."

"Everyone can do with a bit of a rest, I'm sure," said Mooney. "It's been a trying time."

"Freddy! Not me!" squeaked Edith. "You have no idea of my income the last year or two! I don't have your money, Freddy!"

"Indeed not," agreed Mooney.

No one was eating. Moxie had eaten nothing. Koller, McKensie and Littleford had stopped eating, and food was left on their plates. Mooney, however, had cleaned his plate twice.

Mooney blinked his eyes brightly at the group. "Anyone for a drink?"

"Hair of the dog," Koller said to his plate.

"Eye opener," said McKensie.

"Anything," said Edith Howell. "Damn all cows, jumping or otherwise, and their milk!"

"Trying times," said Mooney.

Gerry Littleford said: "Well...whoever was trying to stop this production...succeeded."

32

"If John Meade turns State's Evidence," Fletch asked carefully, "will you drop whatever charges there are outstanding against him?"

He did not know where the police station in Key West was, so he had taken a taxi. He also wanted to be there before too many papers had been filled in regarding Meade, and before too many newspapers had been filled in regarding Meade.

Sergeant Hennings had appeared as soon as Fletch asked the desk man if he could see him.

Apparently the sergeant did not rate an office, maybe not even a desk.

They were sitting on a bench at the side of the police station lobby.

"What evidence?" Sergeant Hennings asked.

"He doesn't have it yet," Fletch answered. "Because I haven't given it to him yet."

"Evidence about what?"

"Look, Sergeant, you didn't raid The Blue House this morning just to bust a beloved movie actor for a few qualudes."

"That's right," the sergeant said. "I didn't." He stood up. "You want some coffee?"

"No thanks."

The sergeant wandered behind the counter and into the backroom. When he returned he had a half-empty Styrofoam cup of coffee in his hand.

"You're saying you think you know something you can use to get Meade off the hook?"

"No," Fletch said. "Sorry. I don't *know* it. I have an idea."

"Why didn't you tell me before? When I was at the house this morning?"

"Because I didn't have the idea this morning. I hadn't noticed something. And I hadn't noticed it because I wasn't suspicious before you showed up."

"You're being mighty foxy."

"No. I'm offering you cooperation."

"For a price."

"John Meade doesn't belong in your jail, and you know it. Everytime you cops bust an admired person for drugs, you're making drug taking seem more admirable, more acceptable, and you know it. You're doing the same thing an advertising agency would be doing hiring John Meade to advertise soft drinks or chewing tobacco."

"So people who are famous shouldn't be arrested?"

"That's not what I'm saying. There are no special rules. I guess. Maybe there are. I don't know. If you've got a real case, you have to do something about it. Otherwise, you've got to look at the end result of what you're doing. Just like everybody else. It's called prudence."

"Busting John Meade is imprudent?"

"It's stupid. It sells drugs. Is it the object of the police to sell drugs?"

"Never heard this argument before."

"Maybe I've been a movie star hanger-on too long. All of three days."

Sergeant Hennings sat down. "What do you want to say?"

"I want to see John Meade."

"Let me see if I've got this right: you want to tell John Meade something he can use to turn state's evidence, as you call it, to get himself off?"

"Right."

"Technically, not correct."

"Sorry."

"In other words, you're saying if we let John Meade go, you'll tell us something that might be useful?"

"Let him go and destroy all papers relating to his ever having been in this police station."

"Why don't you just tell me directly?"

"Why don't you make the damn deal?"

"Oh!" Sergeant Hennings smiled. "Okay."

"Okay?"

"Okay. I swear to it on my grandmother's grave."

"Was your grandmother a nice lady?"

"The best."

"The owner of The Blue House is Ted Sills."

"I know that."

"Ted distinctly did not want to rent The Blue House to me. I forced him. I needed to get Moxie somewhere, not too far away from Fort Myers, where she could recuperate..."

"From Peterman's murder."

"Yeah. Peace and quiet."

"You've had a lot of that."

"Not much. Finally Sills suggested an exorbitant rent. I surprised him by agreeing to it."

"How much?"

"You wouldn't believe. Anyway, as soon as he sees on the television that Frederick and Moxie Mooney are staying in The Blue House and crowds and news cameras are collecting outside, he calls up and starts screaming. He sounds like a puppy with a bone suddenly surrounded by the neighborhood mongrels."

"Can't blame him."

"Sergeant, he doesn't want attention attracted to that house—any kind of attention. He calls time and again, each time getting more shrill, more threatening. Last time he called, he said he was coming after me with a shotgun."

"And yet you stayed."

"I had a choice? How do you move someone like Edith Howell? Getting old Mooney out of a bar requires the tact and logistical brains of an Eisenhower."

"Chuck told me. Threatened him with Jessie James."

"This morning you raided The Blue House."

"And found nothing."

"Glad to hear you say that. After you left, I called Ted Sills. To report to him his house had been raided. Well, sir, he left the country suddenly last night. When he was supposed to be at a horse race today."

"Yeah, Fletcher, you've got the point: we think Sills is a big-volume drug runner. So when are you going to get to the news?"

"It hits me that Ted Sills doesn't want attention drawn to The Blue House because there are drugs in it. This morning you guys searched the place. No drugs."

"No drugs at all."

"Glad to hear you say that." Fletch focused his eyes across the room and blinked. "John Meade going to be released?"

"On my grandmother's grave."

"All reports regarding him destroyed?"

"I'll eat them for lunch. With mayonnaise. Where's the heroin?"

Fletch looked at the sergeant. "I don't really know."

"Great. Why am I sitting here talking to a..."

"A what?"

"I don't know what!"

"During breakfast, I noticed that on the surface of the cistern in the backyard of The Blue House is what looks to me like a trap door. Because of the salt in the air, whatnot, I can't tell if the trap door is newer than the cistern, you know? The lift-rings are rusted. I also don't know how cisterns work."

"They have to be cleaned."

"I do know the Lopezes tell me The Blue House hasn't used cistern water since the water treatment plant was built over on Stock Island."

"Did you lift the hatch and look in the cistern?"

"No."

"Why not?"

"I'm not a cop. Besides," Fletch said, "if I found there weren't any drugs in the cistern, I wouldn't have anything to talk with you about."

"Jeez. No wonder you get along with those flakey movie stars."

"I don't, really. Edith Howell says she'll never visit me again. I'm all broken up about it."

"I bet. She threw an aspirin bottle at Officer Owen King. Raised a welt on his cheek. Would have brought her in for assaulting an officer, but the lady happened to be in bed when she threw the bottle. Actual fact, the incident might have caused titterin' in the courtroom."

"Must maintain the dignity of the fuzz."

"You said it."

"Do I have a good idea?"

"Worth checking out." Sergeant Henning stood up and started to amble toward the back room again.

"Are you bringing Mister Meade out?"

"Sure," Sergeant Henning said, "soon as he finishes autographin' everybody's gunbelts."

33

Fletch stood on the second floor back balcony of The Blue House, his hands on the railing. He was watching the policemen in the backyard. Sergeant Hennings was directing the removal of furniture from the top of the cistern.

Downstairs, in the living room, a morning cocktail party was in progress. Edith Howell, Sy Koller and Frederick Mooney stood in a close triangle, drinks in their hands, drinks in their heads, outshouting reminiscences at each other. *It wasn't Olivier who said that. I was there at the time*... Geoffrey McKensie sat alone at the side of the room, sipping from a glass of dark whiskey. John Meade had gone to the kitchen for a late breakfast or an early lunch. Mrs Lopez said Gerry Littleford had gone to the hospital to collect Stella. Lopez had gone to the hardware store to buy window glass. Moxie was sitting in the bedroom staring at a game show on television.

In the backyard, two policemen lifted the hatch easily. Sergeant Hennings looked down and then knelt down and reached into the cistern. He pulled up one plastic bag. Then another.

He looked up at Fletch on the balcony and gave the thumbs-up sign.

Fletch waved back.

"The fog is beginning to clear." In the bedroom, Fletch flicked off the television. Sitting with her legs in the double width chair, Moxie simply looked at him. "The cops just found a lot of heroin—I guess it is—in the cistern in the backyard."

Her expression remained blank. "Did you help them find it?"

"Sure."

"Why?"

"I don't like heroin. I don't like people who import heroin illegally. I don't like people who sell heroin to other people."

"I don't see how it helps me." Then she shook her head with distaste at what she had just said. "You said I have to think of myself now."

"You do. But things are beginning to become clearer. Listen, Moxie, this is my best guess at the moment." He remained standing in the bedroom. "Steve Peterman and Ted Sills were friends. We knew that. They were also in business together. We didn't know that."

"Smuggling shit."

"Yeah. I would say Sills was on the smuggling end of it; Peterman the financial end. Sills used The Blue House as a stash. Which is why he owns it. Which is why the Lopezes have been so lonely. The house isn't really used for anything else. Except maybe—" Fletch grinned ruefully at himself, "—to entertain damned fools who can be talked into investing in slow race horses. Peterman was moving an awful lot of money around, in and out of the country, from banks in Honduras, Columbia, to banks in Switzerland, France, under the name of Jumping Cow Productions, and, most regrettably, under your own name. Moxie, you were being used like a laundry. An awful lot of money was being washed—at least loosened up, freed, moved—under your name."

"Did they think they could get away with it forever?"

"Moxie, they didn't give one damn about you."

"That's nice."

"I would say that in order to make Jumping Cow Productions continue looking like a viable film company, Peterman ultimately knew he had to make a film. Or appear to be making a film. But a successful film would only draw attention to Jumping Cow Productions."

"So he was purposely making a bad film."

"Purposely."

She sighed. "A film so bad it couldn't even be released."

"It must have blown his mind when Talcott Cross actually hired a good director, Geoff McKensie, who then showed up with a good script."

Moxie almost laughed. "Dear Steve."

"That put him in quite a pickle. He had to get rid of McKensie and bring in a washed-out director who would film a bad script exactly as it was written—badly."

"Okay, okay. Are you saying Sills murdered Peterman?"

"I don't think so."

"Sills wasn't even on location. He couldn't have been."

"He could have had someone get on location and kill Peterman. But why would Sills want to kill Peterman?"

"Trouble between them."

"Clearly, Sills isn't better off with Peterman dead. He hightailed it to France last night. At least the way things have worked out, he isn't better off."

Moxie was distinctly looking tired. "What are you telling me. Fletch?"

"I don't know. Moxie, why the hell did you go along with acting in a bad, offensive movie? You're too good for that."

"I understood there was another script. A good one. McKensie's, I guess. When I arrived in Naples, I understood McKensie was directing. Then things happened awfully fast. McKensie's wife was dead. Koller was directing. We were shooting the original script. The whole film company, the crew were on location. My mind was taken up with where Freddy was, when was *he* going to get run over? What was I supposed to do, walk out? On my own friend-agent-manager-producer?"

"Still—"

"Fletch. Remember the time I had a broken wrist in London?"

"I never knew you had a broken wrist in London."

"I did. I was in the middle of filming *The Face of Things*. I broke my wrist. I was really blue. Steven flew in from somewhere within a matter of hours. Moved me into an even more expensive, more comfortable suite at the Montcalm. Surrounded me with flowers. Smoothed out all the contract nonsense. Got a special, removable cast rigged for my wrist. Showed them all how we could continue filming even if I did have a broken wrist."

"You filmed *The Face of Things* with a broken wrist?"

"About half of it. See it sometime. In about half the film, I don't use my left hand at all."

"And you're saying Peterman's doing all that was some kind of a favor?"

"Seemed so at the time."

"How's your left wrist?"

She wriggled it. "I have almost full use of it."

"Some favor."

"I needed the money. A lot of people were able to keep working."

"Yeah, you're really well off now. Peterman saw to that, all right. Terrific guy."

"Oh, Fletch!"

"Don't get angry with me."

"Well, what's all this supposed to come down to? I'm a fool, I'm a murderer, and now I'm some kind of big gangster? Now I'm responsible for scrambling the brains of half the people in the country?"

"Not half."

"Any people?" Tears rolled down Moxie's cheeks. "What good does all this do me? Next to me, Eva Braun looks like Madame Curie!"

The phone rang twice. They ignored it.

"Take it easy, Moxie. I'm just reporting that we're coming to some sort of an understanding of what happened. We know more than we did."

"You're just getting me in worse trouble! I'm an innocent person! I didn't kill anybody! I don't know anything about this business! I don't know anything about drugs!"

Quietly, Fletch said, "I think if Peterman were alive, I'd kill the son of a bitch."

"Terrific! So I did, right?"

"You had plenty reason to."

"Well, I didn't." Leaning forward, she dried her tears on her linen jacket. "Here I am, sitting in this stupid house, crying my eyes out, people throwing rocks—"

"Sy Koller knows all about this funny money movie business. I've talked to him. I wonder to what extent he was in on all this. He knew Peterman and Buckley were in some sort of a deal together."

"Go get Sy Koller arrested. He can direct his own execution. That way it will never come off."

There was a knock on the door.

Lopez was in the corridor. "Chief..."

"Nachman?"

"The police. On the phone. She says she must speak to you."

"Okay. I'll take the call downstairs."

In the bedroom, Moxie had gotten up from her chair and clicked on the television set. Noon weather was being reported. The report was that it was a nice day.

Koller had just climbed the stairs. He was a little out of breath. His black T-shirt was more than usually strained.

In the corridor, Fletch said to him, "Sy, that story you told me the other night. Was it last night? About that fight you and Peterman had."

Koller was looking with big eyes at Fletch from close-up. Fletch could smell the liquor on his breath.

"You said Peterman was putting up phony movies and pocketing the money he raised. But you knew he was actually concealing the movement of drug money around the world. Right?"

Koller raised his hand as if to grab something at eye level. "That's how I had him by the short hairs."

Koller lumbered down the corridor toward his room.

"Sy? You knew *Midsummer Night's Madness* was never going to be released..."

At his door, Koller turned around. "Anything for a job, boy. Anything for a week's pay."

He closed the door behind him.

34

"And how's the weather on Bonita Beach now?" Fletch said into the phone. "Still photogenic?"

"I'm not in Fort Myers," Chief of Detectives Roz Nachman said. "I'm at the airport in Key West. And I've put my last coin into the phone box waiting for you to pick up the phone."

"Sorry. Catching the noon weather report on television."

"I'm waiting to be picked up by the local force."

"They've had a busy morning. Up early, rousting the citizens—"

"I called you earlier, before I left the office but someone insisted you weren't there."

"I was helping the police on an underground matter. You have news?"

"Just keep everybody at the house until I arrive, please."

"What's your news?"

"If everybody isn't there when I arrive, I'll hold you responsible, Mister Fletcher."

"Did Steve Peterman rent a car before he rented the car you examined?"

Nachman paused. "Yes. An identical blue Cadillac. From another company. The day of the accident, he turned one car in at the airport, leaving it in the parking lot, and rented another one."

"And was the first car damaged?"

"Yes."

"Had it been in a hit-and-run accident?"

"Yes. Blood, bits of cloth beneath the front fender. The fender itself had been washed off."

"The blood match?"

"We're presuming it does. We'll know soon. There's a police car. I'd better go outside so they'll see me. Don't let anybody leave, Fletcher."

"We'll be glad to see you, Chief. At least I will."

35

Upstairs, Fletch went back into the bedroom and closed the door. The television was still running, softly. On a women's talk show, herpes was being discussed.

Fletch sat in the double width chair with Moxie. He took her hand.

"Nachman is on her way over from the airport," Fletch said. "To arrest Geoffrey McKensie for the murder of Steven Peterman."

The television was telling women not to feel badly about having herpes.

"Peterman killed McKensie's wife," Fletch said. "Ran her down with a rented blue Cadillac."

Again tears were rolling down Moxie's cheeks.

"You see," Fletch said, "Koller was right: McKensie did know how to rig a set."

Moxie freed her hand. She stood up. She walked to the bed and sat on its edge.

She sobbed.

Fletch grabbed a tissue from the bedside table and handed it to her. "I'd think you'd be relieved."

"Poor Geoff." She blew her nose. "Poor damn Geoff. Why did they have to find out?"

She began to choke. She went into the bathroom. She closed the door.

Fletch listened to her sobbing and blowing her nose and sobbing some more.

"I'll be downstairs," he said to the closed door.

36

Mrs Lopez opened the front door of The Blue House when the police arrived. Fletch was in the living room, within sight of the front door. He had walked around the house seeing where everyone was.

Chief of Detectives Roz Nachman entered. Sergeant Hennings was behind her.

Fletch shook hands with them. "McKensie is in the small library at the back of the house. Trying to arrange a flight to Sydney."

Nachman said: "Good."

"Having a busy day, Sergeant."

"Busier than some."

Moxie came down the stairs. She had put on the white linen trousers and the sandals Fletch had bought her. Obviously she had washed her face with cold water, but her eyes still showed she had been crying.

"Hello, Chief," she said.

Chief Nachman said to her: "You have the right to remain silent—"

"What!" Fletch yelled.

"Will you please allow me to finish reciting this lady her rights?"

"You're arresting Moxie?"

"If you'd stop making so much noise."

"But you can't!"

"I can. I should. I must. I am arresting Ms Moxie Mooney for the murder of Steven Peterman."

Frederick Mooney stood in the living room door. His eyes were hollow, empty.

"Geoff McKensie killed Peterman!" Fletch exclaimed. He looked around. McKensie was standing down the corridor outside the billiard room door. "Peterman killed McKensie's wife!"

"Sorry, Mister McKensie," Nachman said. "You didn't know that before, did you?"

In the shadow of the deep corridor, McKensie's ruddy complexion paled.

"Of course he knew it!" insisted Fletch.

"He wasn't even on location that day, Mister Fletcher. Not in the afternoon. He was in Miami, seeing lawyers."

"I saw him at the police station."

"He was at the police station, yes. He heard the news on the car radio and came directly to the police station. He was not on location."

"He rigged the set."

"The set was not rigged," said Nachman. "So say the experts."

"God," said Fletch.

Nachman fully recited Moxie Mooney her rights. To Fletch, it sounded like the mumblings over a grave. Staring at Nachman, Moxie's eyes were glazed. Mrs Lopez' face was long. In the living room doorway Mooney swayed stupidly. Down the corridor, McKensie was leaning against a table.

"What evidence?" Fletch asked lamely.

"Cut it out, Fletcher," Nachman said, as if admonishing a child. "All the evidence in the world. Motive: we've had a report on her financial records. Whatever swindles Moxie and Peterman were pulling, it had certainly gone sour for Moxie. Opportunity: she was on the stage with him; she was wearing a bulky bathrobe in which a knife could be easily concealed; she crossed behind him just as he was stabbed. Dan Buckley was also on the stage, but there was no way he could have concealed that knife in his clothes, and he never left his chair. Motive and opportunity make the case."

Silently, looking as if he were going someplace to be sick, Frederick Mooney crossed the front hall to the stairs. His fingers just barely touched Moxie's sleeve.

Her eyes watched him climb the stairs.

Sergeant Hennings released handcuffs from his belt. He said to Fletch: "Okay if I arrest her? She's talented and famous."

"It's not okay!" Fletch shouted. "No handcuffs!"

263

"Sorry, Miss," Hennings said to Moxie. "Police department rules."

"Don't I get to get my toothbrush?" Moxie asked.

"We supply toothbrushes now," Nachman said. "Especially for capital offenses."

Moxie held out her wrists. Moxie Mooney was looking drawn and haggard.

She smiled at Fletch. "What's your line about bravery?"

Fletch answered numbly, "Bravery is something you have to think you have to have it."

"Yeah," Moxie said. "I'll think on that."

"I'm going with you," Fletch said.

Roz Nachman said, "Sorry, earwig, you're not. Not enough room in the helicopter."

Sergeant Hennings was guiding Moxie through the front door, gently, by her elbow.

Moxie was looking back at Fletch. "Hey, Fletch?" she asked. "You've never told me. Here's your chance. Why is this house called The Blue House?"

Nachman put her nose up at the corners of the ceilings. "Used to be a whore house," she said.

"Really?" Fletch said. "I never knew that."

In the front hall, Fletch turned in a complete circle.

McKensie approached. Bitterly he said to Fletch, "Thanks, mate."

Then he went up the stairs.

From the front porch of The Blue House Fletch watched them put Moxie in the police car. Chief of Detectives Roz Nachman got in the back seat with her.

He watched the car drive off.

He stared at where the car had been. *Moxie...
fun and games...so many images of Moxie...on this
beach and that beach...in the street...in the classroom
...in little theaters...in this room and that...getting
into the back of a police car in handcuffs.*

Behind him, Mrs Lopez said, "Can I get you
something, Mister Fletcher? Maybe a drink...?"

He said: "Apple juice."

She said, "We don't have apple juice."

"You don't?" He turned to her.

"We never have apple juice. Why have apple
juice in the land of orange juice?"

Fletch stared at her.

"I can make you a nice rum drink with orange
juice."

"Excuse me."

Fletch went by her and up the stairs.

37

Fletch knocked on Frederick Mooney's bedroom door and entered without waiting to be invited.

Mooney was sitting in a Morris chair, his hands in his lap. Silently, he watched Fletch.

"How long you been sober?" Fletch asked.

"Over three years."

The airlines flight bag was on the floor beside the bed. Fletch hunkered down next to it. He lifted one of the bottles from it. He uncapped the bottle and sniffed the contents.

"You can't get apple juice in most bars," Mooney said.

Fletch left the bottle on the bureau. "You're one hell of an actor."

"I thought you knew that." Mooney shifted in

his chair. "Of course I had the advantage. Once people think of you as a drunk, they see you as a drunk."

"Moxie said you were drunk when she arrived at her apartment in New York."

"I had set the stage, knowing she'd show up sometime. Empty bottles around, dirty smelly glasses..."

"But why?"

"I wanted to see her, as it were, without being seen. She would have shut off the reformed Frederick Mooney. I had shut her off too many years. Her behavior would have been cool and proper in front of the great man, her father. I decided the best way to see her, to really see her, get to know her, was as a dependent. In front of a helpless old man, blind drunk, Marilyn was herself. I've really gotten to know her, the last few weeks. She's really quite marvelous."

"But she hasn't gotten to know you."

"It doesn't matter," said Frederick Mooney. "It's all on film."

"So at the apartment in New York you heard everything. Everything about Peterman—"

"Of course. I even read *Midsummer Night's Madness* one afternoon while she was out. I knew the fiddle was on. You see, Fletch..." Fletch, in continued shock, glanced at the man. He could not get his mind around the dimensions of this man's acting genius. All that Peterman-Peterkin-Peterson-Patterson routine had been consciously created. "...in my twenties, I was virtually ruined by one of these charlatan friend-managers, the word *friend*

267

italicised. I was dragged through courts for five years. Someone I had trusted. It virtually ruined my work, my sleep, my health. One is made to feel so vulnerable, so weak. And doing creative work while being made to feel weak and vulnerable is immensely hard. Mind breaking. Creative people should receive some protection by law. There really aren't that many of us, and our time is short, our energies limited. Our energies should not be drained by lawyers playing at their paper games. Something similiar happened to me again in my late thirties. If I had known then what I know now—that energies do not last forever—I would have killed anyone who so assaulted me."

"Instead you killed Steve Peterman."

"I haven't been able to do much for Moxie, as a father. I didn't want her to be dragged through the courts for years, humiliated, made a fool, her life and work laid out in little boxes, her every privacy invaded. Preventing all that was something I could do for her."

"How did you do it?"

"I'm an actor. A well-trained actor."

"You know how to ride a horse like a guardsman and an Indian, how to handle a gun as if it were a natural extention of your hand..."

"You heard that little sermon I gave at Durty Harry's." Mooney's eyes wandered over the palm trees outside the windows. "Always used to go over well at colleges."

"Downstairs just now," Fletch said, "when they were carting Moxie away, I remembered her telling me, years ago, that as a kid in the carnivals, whatever, small-town travelling shows, you were even a part of a knife throwing act. That was just after I realized I had seen three empty apple juice bottles in the rubbish."

"You'd be surprised how your youthful physical skills come back to you after you've become absolutely tea-total." Mooney smiled. "I was never the drinker I was made out to be, anyway. I cultivated the image. I could heighten the audience's suspense by making them wonder if I was too drunk to go on, too drunk to finish the play. I believe Kean used the same trick. *There's old Mooney, drunk again. It can't be him who's acting so beautifully, but some god acting through him.* You see, everyone had seen *Hamlet* before, knew the story. They had to be made unsure as to whether Mooney could play *Hamlet*. Again. And again and again. Believe me, friend and lover of my daughter, no one could do what I've done as drunk as I'm supposed to have been. Of course I didn't make twenty or thirty pictures without knowing what I was doing. People will believe anything…"

"Mister Mooney, how did you actually commit the murder? There were cameras everywhere."

"I made myself into a rubbish man. A few rags, more hair, more beard, a discouraged way of standing, walking, wandering around location picking up the odd candy wrapper, cigarette pack." He chuckled. "Edith Howell asked me to move a trash barrel away from her trailer. Didn't ask. Demanded. Called me a lazy old lout, when I moved slowly on my supposedly sore feet. Not a very nice lady, Edith Howell."

"She has her eyes on your millions."

"She was always looking the wrong direction onstage, too. She'd look a meter more upstage than she was supposed to be looking, a meter more downstage. That woman drove me nuts all during *Time, Gentlemen, Time*."

"And have you millions of dollars?"

"Sure."

"Many millions?"

"Why not? I've practiced a rewarding profession. Worked hard all my life, and been well paid for it. Never had expensive tastes. One hotel room is very much like another."

"Oh. Moxie thinks you're broke."

"It's been good for her soul to think so."

Fletch sighed.

"So," Mooney continued, "as an old, tolerated member of the custodial staff, I even watched them build the set for *The Dan Buckley Show*. You think I don't know how to work out camera angles? I approached the slit curtain at the back of the set from all the way down the beach, from the water's edge. I had to walk in a very carefully worked-out Z. I never showed up on film. And thankfully there wasn't much breeze. The curtain stayed more or less still."

"Why did you throw the knife into Peterman's back just after Moxie walked behind him?"

"Did I? I didn't know that. I wasn't watching, you see, I couldn't without being seen. I threw the knife at exactly that moment the breeze split the curtain."

"And then walked in a Z back to the water's edge."

"Yes. And by the time you found me in that bar I had been doing my drunk act for a good two hours or more. And I had convinced the bartender that I was drunk when I arrived."

"And no one thought you capable of such a thing."

"Not even you."

"And how did you get on and off location so easily?"

"After all," said Frederick Mooney, "I am Frederick Mooney."

"Yeah. I've heard."

"Making me stop and identify myself, sign in, sign out—really. Not all the rules have to apply to me, you know."

Fletch shook his head and chuckled. "There is a big black dog named Emperor who goes in and out of Durty Harry's. I went back the next night. I had thought it was something you had seen instead of a pink elephant."

"Fletch...it is all right if I call you Fletch, isn't it?"

"I don't know. I was getting sort of used to Peterkin."

"Would you mind having a drink with me?"

"Are you serious?"

"In that flight bag there's another bottle. The real stuff. There are two glasses in the bathroom."

"Sure."

When he was done pouring the drinks Fletch left that bottle on the bureau, too. He handed one glass to Mooney.

"Here's to you, Mister Mooney. It's real interesting knowing you."

"Here's to you, Mister Fletcher. You tried your best, I think."

After the cognac cleared in Fletch's throat, he asked, "Did you mean to get away with it?"

"No." Mooney seemed quite certain on that point. "Of course I expected to be found out."

"Then why did you commit such a clever crime?"

"I like doing things well. Furthermore, puzzling everyone has given me a little more time with Marilyn. Not much."

"What did you expect to do once you were found out?"

"Fade into the background, Fletch, fade into the background. Disguise myself as a pink-kneed, short-pants tourist, or an aged beach bum, or a bewhiskered priest, and slither into the common human pool. I rather fancied retirement for myself in some out of the way place within walking distance of a good, warm, friendly pub, where people care not for theater or films."

"You can't do that now. They've arrested Moxie."

"I couldn't do that anyway, now, you bastard." Mooney grinned ruefully. "You ruined that. You put me on an airplane and landed me on a spit of sand at the end of the world. There's no way off Key West for Frederick Mooney. Frederick Mooney couldn't charter a boat or a plane out of Key West disguised as a bedbug. Such people look too closely at you. The first night I was here I went out to investigate. And found there was no way off this damn place for me. I walked so much, I got so tired, I went into a bar and did my drunk act. Had the cops drive me home. One road out of here, and Edith Howell has told me about all those bridges between here and the mainland." Affection was in Mooney's look and his chuckle. "You bastard."

"Sorry. Do you know Peterman killed McKensie's wife? Ran her down with a car."

"Doesn't surprise me. He was wrecking a lot of people, and would wreck many more. What was this all about? A drug scam?"

"Yeah."

"Well," said Mooney, "when the corner candy and newspaper store isn't selling candy and newspapers, you know it must be in some other business."

Fletch put his empty glass on the bureau. "Guess you and I have to fly back to Fort Myers together."

Mooney said, "We don't want to keep Marilyn under duress too long."

"By the way," Fletch asked. "Why didn't you come clean downstairs—before they took her away?"

"Would you believe I was stunned? I had heard so many murder theories floating around, I thought we had plenty more time to be together. I didn't know that Moxie had crossed behind Peterman. Truly stunned. I couldn't think how to handle it downstairs. Here I had successfully passed myself off as a sick old man. What was I supposed to say— *I'm sober and I did it*? Moxie would have said, *Oh, hell!*"

"O.L."

"It will take them a moment to believe this one.

The curtains will have to close and the lights will have to come up. Young man, I know my audience."

Fletch said, "I'll go phone around to charter a plane."

Mooney's empty glass was on the arm rest of his chair. His fingers were folded in his lap.

At the door, Fletch said, "One more question, Mister Mooney. When you and I first met, in that bar on the beach, you told me that Moxie—Marilyn—might have murdered someone, a teacher, a drama coach, when she was fourteen."

Mooney nodded.

"Why did you tell me that—if you knew she hadn't killed Peterman?"

"To keep suspicion—particularly your suspicion—away from me. I knew Marilyn had sent for you. I knew who you are—an old friend and lover of Marilyn's. I knew it would be most difficult for you to believe Marilyn guilty of murder. I made it easier for you. I planted a doubt in your mind."

"You blinded me," Fletch said. "I haven't thought straight since." Fletch's hand was on the door knob. "What was true about the story—anything?"

"Did you ask Marilyn about it?"

"Yes."

"And did she assure you she did not kill Mister Hodes?"

"No. She didn't."

"Ah, that Marilyn." Smiling, Mooney shook his head. "She sure knows how to keep an audience."

38

It took Fletch longer than he expected to charter a plane to Fort Myers. He finally found a charter service in Miami willing to fly down to Key West to pick them up. It would be a while before the plane arrived.

Going back into the front hall, Fletch saw through the open front door that Geoffrey McKensie was in the street putting his luggage into the small yellow car.

A dozen or so people were watching the house from across the street.

Fletch went out to the sidewalk. He stood quietly a moment. Then he said to McKensie: "I'm sorry everything has worked out so rotten for you."

A garbage truck went by. Painted on its side was WE CATER WEDDINGS.

His head in the trunk, McKensie said, "Every time us Aussies leave Australia we get used as cannon fodder."

"History doesn't say so."

McKensie slammed the trunk. "You won't see this lad on these shores again."

"Sorry you feel that way. You ran up against one cheap crook, a murderer—"

"That's not all, brother." McKensie got into the car, closed the door, rolled down the window, started the engine. "I've had my experience with the American film industry. My first and my last."

He drove off.

In the front hall, Edith Howell said, "I'm so sorry, Fletcher. Geoff told us all about the police dragging Moxie away. Not that I blame her for doing in that Steve Peterman. Awful man! I always said so, didn't I, John?" John Meade had carried luggage down the stairs. Stella and Gerry Littleford were coming down the stairs with luggage, as was Sy Koller. Everyone was carrying luggage except Edith Howell. "We were just hoping she'd have a little more time before she was incarcerated. She's been working so hard."

In the street a rubber-neck wagon was going by.... *arrested this afternoon the actress, Moxie Mooney, for first-degree murder. Another tale of Key West...*

Fletch decided not to trouble anyone with the facts. Let these people go. Getting Frederick Mooney

276

out of the house and to the airport would be much easier without his being encircled by the shock and clucking of these people.

"Where's Freddy?" Edith asked. "Getting as drunk as he can as fast as he can, I expect."

"Maybe."

"Oh, I know my Freddy," said Edith. "I wouldn't have that man for all his millions. Scrambled eggs for brains."

"You'd get employed faster, Edith, as Mrs Frederick Mooney," Sy Koller said.

All the people carrying luggage were trying to get around the person not carrying luggage. Edith Howell centered herself nicely in the front hall.

"I don't think Freddy's the great actor people make him out to be, either," said Edith. "In *Time, Gentlemen, Time,* he jumped on my every line. Most annoying. 'Course I knew how much he wanted to get back to his dressing room for a drink."

Fletch watched them go through the process of leaving. It was as if they were leaving a hotel. Edith Howell jabbered to John Meade about getting to Miami, *over those bridges,* before dark. The Littlefords said they had to go back to Vanderbilt Beach where they had left luggage. Sy Koller was grumbling that he supposed he had to go back to Bonita Beach to oversee the shutting down of the *Midsummer Night's Madness* location. "If I don't at least go through the motions," Sy said, "I suppose I'll never get employed again." Stella Littleford carried her bandaged head stiffly and said nothing. Only John Meade shook hands and said good bye and said thank you.

Before getting into the car Gerry Littleford said, "Oh, yeah. Fletch. Someone called. With an English accent. Didn't catch the name. Talked fast. I didn't know where you were. He said to tell you Scarlet something-or-other, Pumpernickle? won a twenty-five thousand dollar purse."

"No foolin'."

"Didn't know you were into horse racing."

"Didn't know Scarlet Pimple-Nickel was either."

If he were a doorman, they might have tipped him. As it was, they all drive off in two cars, discouraged for the moment, Fletch believed, but only for the moment, nevertheless sure that on some tomorrow the right material and the right people would come together and they would create an unreality more credible than reality, and be paid, and be applauded.

39

This time after knocking on Frederick Mooney's bedroom door, Fletch waited to be invited in. There was no response. He knocked again.

He opened the door.

Frederick Mooney was on his back on the bed. On the bedside table were a drinking glass and one of the bottles, three-quarters full.

Fletch closed the door and went to the bedside. "Mister Mooney?"

He shook the man's arm. "Oh, come on. I don't need a final act."

He sniffed the bottle on the bedside table. Cognac

"Come on," said Fletch. "I'm sure you can also hold your breath and play dead longer than anyone else who's ever been on the stage."

On the bed the other side of Mooney was an empty tablet bottle. The cap was off. Fletch reached over Mooney and picked up the bottle. The label was for prescription sleeping tablets.

"Mister Mooney!" Fletch said. "You set the stage nicely. Now let's go."

He shook him again. "Jeez," Fletch said. "Do I believe it?"

He felt for the pulse in Mooney's wrist. There was none. Frederick Mooney was not breathing at all.

"O.L.!" Fletch dropped Mooney's hand. "God-damn it, now you're not acting at all!"

A curtain of wetness slipped down over Fletch's eyes. The afternoon light from the windows was bright.

On the desk were two envelopes and an open note. Fletch went to the desk. The two envelopes were sealed. One said, *Ms Marilyn Mooney*; the other, *The Authorities*.

The open note was to him.

Fletcher,

"If I may ask you to do us one more favor? Please deliver these notes as addressed.

The letter to the authorities describes how and why I killed Steven Peterman in such detail that they will have no choice but to believe me. My doctor will testify that I have been tea-total since I developed a heart problem more than three years ago, and I have provided the authorities with his name.

The letter to Marilyn cannot explain all. Perhaps you can help her to understand. It says I have enjoyed spending these weeks with her, watching her, applauding her, loving her from behind the curtain, as it were. I am also telling her that I am leaving her enough money so that she certainly should be able to pay off all these financial charges against her, however great, and maybe have enough left over for a quiet, non-working weekend sometime in her life.

I am reminded now of all the thousands of nights I have left some theater somewhere, tired to the bones, and walked alone to some hotel, only perchance to sleep, wondering as I walked why such talents, such expertise, such energy is spent creating an illusion for a handful of people, for a few hours. What for? One can suspend reality, but never conquer it.

Thanks for having me.

Frederick Mooney

40

In the quiet house, Fletch went back downstairs, along the corridor, through the billiard room and into the small library at the back of the house.

He sat at the desk.

He called Chief of Detectives Roz Nachman's telephone number and left the message asking her to return the call immediately upon her arrival.

He called Miami and enquired about the airplane he had chartered. It had already left. He asked the dispatcher to radio the pilot that now Fletch would need the airplane for a return flight to Fort Myers.

Then, for the first time, Fletch remembered that days before he had abandoned a rented car at

Fort Myers airport. His luggage was still in the car.

Then he called Washington, D.C. Now was the time to see if Global Cable News would listen to just any *barefoot boy with cheek* who happened to have a story.

A woman answered, saying, "Good afternoon. Global News. May I help you?"

"Hello," Fletch said. "My name is Armistad..."

DIRTY HARRY by Dane Hartman

He's "Dirty Harry" Callahan—tough, unorthodox, no-nonsense plain-clothesman extraordinaire of the San Francisco Police Department...inspector #71 assigned to the bruising, thankless homicide detail...A consummate crimebuster nothing can stop—not even the law! Explosive mysteries involving racketeers, murderers, extortioners, pushers, and skyjackers: savage, bizarre murders, accomplished with such cunning and expertise that the frustrated S.F.P.D. finds itself without a single clue; hair-raising action and violence as Dirty Harry arrives on the scene, armed with nothing but a Smith & Wesson .44 and a bag of dirty tricks; unbearable suspense and hairy chase sequences as Dirty Harry sleuths to unmask the villain and solve the mystery. Dirty Harry—when the chips are down, he's the most low-down cop on the case.

MYSTERY...SUSPENSE...ESPIONAGE

__**THE GOLD CREW**
*by Thomas N. Scortia
& Frank M. Robinson*   (B83-522, $2.95)
The most dangerous test the world has ever known is now
taking place aboard the mammoth nuclear sub *Alaska*.
Human beings, unpredictable in moments of crisis, are
being put under the ultimate stress. On patrol, out of con-
tact with the outside world, the crew is deliberately being
led to believe that the U.S.S.R. has attacked the U.S.A.
Will the crew follow standing orders and fire the *Alaska's*
missiles in retaliation? Now the fate of the world depends
on what's going on in the minds of the men of THE GOLD
CREW.

__**YESTERDAY'S SPY**
by Len Deighton   (B31-014, $2.50)
Two friends who spied together. But that was in another
time and another place—now they fight on different sides.
A spellbinding tale of deceit and terror in a world where
political reality destroys the most hallowed allegiances.

__**THE HAMLET ULTIMATUM**
by Leonard Sanders   (B83-461, $2.95)
World takeover is HAMLET's goal! The mysterious terrorist
group has already sabotaged all the computer networks it
requires, even that of the C.I.A. Now the group is ready for
its ultimatum to the U.S. government: Surrender or watch
the entire Northeast burn in a nuclear disaster. Only ex-
agent Loomis can stop them. And only Loomis and his
team have the courage to oppose the President and fight
the world they want to save.

MYSTERY...INTRIGUE...SUSPENSE

FLETCH AND THE WIDOW BRADLEY
by Gregory Mcdonald   (B90-922, $2.95)
Fletch has got *some* trouble! Body trouble: with an executive dead in Switzerland. His ashes shipped home prove it. Or do they? Job trouble: When Fletch's career is ruined for the mistake no reporter should make. Woman trouble: with a wily widow and her suspect sister-in-law. From Alaska to Mexico, Fletch the laid-back muckraker covers it all!